FREDERICA'S OUTLAW

RAIN TRUEAX

Frederica's Outlaw

Hunters Moon ,The Taggerts, Book 8
is an original work of Rain Trueax.

Originally released 2016 as Sonoran Christmas.
Edited and retitled 1-2020

ISBN 978-1-943537-59-4

Prepared and presented by:
Seven Oaks
Monmouth, OR
Tucson, AZ

-012720-112-

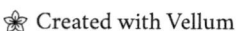 Created with Vellum

INTRODUCTION

Sometimes a simple, "Can I help you Ma'am" changes the way the world turns. So, it was for fine Bostonian, Frederica Windsor and crusty, Jeremiah Taggert, a total surprise when a spark was struck changing both their worlds. Frederica's Outlaw, a novella of discovery, adventure and romance that blossoms in the later years. Building on characters from the earlier Arizona historicals and starting a foundation for the themes of the contemporary Barrio Viejo, Mystic Shadows Series.

Read the Taggert, Hunters Moon, Arizona historicals and the Barrio Viejo stories and e-mail me (raintrueax@gmail.com) with your guesses on how this all worked out. The bridge story starts in 1906 with a catastrophic event that levels all people and opens a track for a whole new set of adventure romances.

CHAPTER 1

December 20, 1905

Frederica Jamison Lawrence Windsor descended the steps from her private car to the Tucson platform. Looking around the city, she was unsure what to make of what seemed a foreign environment. This was a week before Christmas. Where was the snow? There were some decorations, a few windows with greens, but nothing like Boston before she had departed.

She felt dusty, more than a little wilted from days on the train where even her private car did little to lessen the misery. Would anyone ever fix the tracks out in this godforsaken part of the country? Her sixty-year old back might never recover.

A porter carried her bags from the car but left them stacked beside her. She looked at him with shock as he walked off. How was she supposed to get them from the platform to her hotel room? She went into the depot to see a bored looking man behind a desk. "I need to get myself and my bags to the Santa Rita Hotel." He looked at her and yawned. "Naturally, I would pay for the assistance", she said lifting her receptacle to indicate her source of funds.

He turned and looked behind him. "George, can you help this lady?"

A skinny old man looked around the clerk and nodded. "You need a buggy?" he asked.

"How many blocks would it be?" She knew she looked old. Did she also look incapable of walking a few blocks?

She saw them both consider. "About five or maybe six," the skinny man said. He looked at the other man, rubbing his head. "Think it might be seven?"

"More'n likely."

So, they didn't know. She regretted allowing Wilson, her major-domo to remain in El Paso to visit with his family. She had thought the worst of her travel would be over by then.

"I will need help getting my bags there," she said thinking neither of the gentlemen looked more capable of carrying them than she was. Perhaps she did need a buggy. Did Tucson have hacks?

"May I help you, ma'am?" a deep voice asked from behind her. She turned to see a tall, black-haired man with gray in hair and mustache. He swept off his hat and smiled. Good Lord, was that a gun on his hip? She had believed Tucson was becoming more civilized. Hadn't she read that the city had made gambling illegal? Surely, they did not permit guns on their streets.

"I can manage," Something about the man made her uneasy. She tried to put her finger on it, and then realized he looked like the outlaws on the covers of books she read before leaving Boston. She had assumed them fictional—even if they were entertaining. Weren't gunmen a thing of the past?

"Fine. I'm here to pick up a shipment." He looked to the clerk. "Did it come in, Ralph?"

Ralph nodded. "Out on the platform."

The tall man look back at her. "I have a buggy. Won't take me out of my way to get you to your hotel." That was not happening. Getting in a buggy with a possible outlaw. Not on her life. Who knew where she'd end up?

"Ma'am ..maybe you'd like to call whoever you came to meet in Tucson."

"This was to be a surprise." Not necessarily a pleasant one either, as she didn't expect her daughter to be pleased to see her.

"My name is Jeremiah, Mrs…" He stopped and looked at her expectantly.

"Windsor."

"All right then, Mrs. Windsor. "I can get you and your bags to the Santa Rita Hotel, or you can leave your trunks here, and hope they are still here when the hotel sends back someone to retrieve them."

"Jeremiah's a reliable man," Ralph said, with a chuckle, "Now."

The tall man gave him a glare that quieted the chuckle. "I'll stop by the hotel and tell 'em to send someone over for you," he drawled, then grinned. "Since you're clear afraid of going a few blocks with me."

She knew what he was doing but didn't care. She'd already decided she was being a fool not to accept his offer. It was broad daylight. Hardly a risk for a few blocks—even if this town did have a very western feel to it. She carried a derringer in her receptacle. She could protect herself if the need arose.

A few moments later, he had loaded her trunks, his boxes, and helped her into the buggy. "You don't look much like the sort of lady I'd expect to be stopping in Tucson," he said without looking at her, as he expertly flicked the reins. His hands were large, dusted lightly with hair. Despite the fact, he clearly was not young, he was a powerful looking man. She found him surprisingly fascinating for reasons that probably went back to those silly books.

"I had my reasons," she said when she realized he was waiting for a response.

"Traveling alone too."

"I had my aide, Wilson, with me as far as El Paso. He'll arrive here in a few days."

"You coming to have Christmas with family?"

"Is that your business?"

He chuckled. "Nah. You sure you don't want me to notify whoever you are coming to meet?" he asked as he stopped the buggy in front of a large hotel.

"No, thank you."

He jumped down, secured the reins to a post, helped her to alight, and carried her trunks into the lobby.

"How ya doin', Taggert?" the clerk asked and then looked twice as he saw her for the first time. "Can I help ya, ma'am?"

Jeremiah hadn't given her his last name. Why did it sound familiar? She put the question aside for considering later. "I am Mrs. Windsor. I believe you have a suite reserved for me."

The clerk grinned widely as he looked behind him for keys. "I do indeed. Your room is on the third floor. Would you like help with your bags?" He pointed to a lift at the other end of the lobby. She was surprised to see such a modern convenience. "Yes, I'd appreciate that."

The clerk hit the bell. In moments, a young man appeared. He acquired a cart and with Jeremiah's help put everything on it. She turned then to the tall man. "I appreciate your help." She reached into her bag for a tip, but he put out his hand to stop her. How rude.

"No need for that. Just glad to be of use." His eyes had a glint that she couldn't quite decipher, as he tipped his hat and strode out of the hotel.

"You know the man it seems," she said looking at the clerk.

"Pretty much everybody knows Taggert and his boys." The clerk grinned.

She debated asking more questions but decided against it as she followed the bellboy to the lift and her room on the third floor.

The suite had a lovely décor, a large window overlooked a garden far below. She opened the window as the young man set her trunks near a large cupboard. She handed him a generous tip. "Does the hotel have a maid service?" she asked.

He nodded. "I'll send Nelly to you."

When he was gone, she made sure the telephone worked, took the hatpin from her bonnet and set it on the dresser. Staring at her reflection in the mirror, she tried to be unbiased. Her hair had once been black. Now it was streaked with silver. She peered closer to see fine lines around her eyes. For a sixty year old woman, she looked healthy… she thought. The trip had worn her out, and a good sleep would do much to restore her normal vigor. Finding her daughter would do even more.

Again, she asked herself why Cat had left Boston without a word, telling no one. Had she felt threatened by someone? Why hadn't she confided in her? Most likely because she thought her mother would try to stop her or was it that she was angry at her and hadn't wanted to say? But angry about what? She had to stop asking herself such questions. The answers had to come from Cat.

An hour later, Nelly, freckled, curly haired, and full of energy, had arrived, unpacked her gowns, and hung them on hangers, folding her other garments in drawers. "I may need a maid while in town as mine had no interest in following me west. Do you know of anyone?" she asked, handing the young woman a gratuity.

"Would it be for long, ma'am?"

"I am not sure. A month perhaps. I plan to stay here until at least after the New Year."

"I'll ask around, ma'am."

"Have you lived here long, Nelly?"

"Five years now."

"I was looking for my daughter who would have arrived possibly two months ago. Catherine Lawrence, red-haired, about my height."

"Doesn't sound familiar. I can ask around though if you'd like."

"I would." She smiled. "Thank you."

"My pleasure. Merry Christmas, ma'am." With that, the young woman was gone.

Merry Christmas indeed. She wondered when she had last had one. Losing a son and a husband in a tragic accident, a second husband to illness, she had nothing anywhere if Cat had left with the intended purpose of cutting her off. She unbuttoned and removed her gown, grateful she didn't need a maid for such services, and lay on the bed, trying to decide how she would find her daughter. Maybe the detective had been wrong, and she hadn't gone to Tucson, or maybe she had already gone on. She stared blankly at the ceiling. What then?

She was sure there had been such times, but she didn't remember the years she had celebrated Christmas with joy. It had been good when Catherine was a baby and Jacob had been old enough to know what it all meant. She smiled at the memory, though she usually blocked such from her mind. Live in the present. Don't bemoan what had been lost. Wealthy as she was, with all the benefits of such resources, none of them could bring back her dead son.

With his father, her six-year-old son had gone for a boat ride into the sea, a calm sea, except it had not stayed that way. When the storm blew up, seemingly from nowhere, she had held her baby in her arms waiting, praying, hoping. It was all for naught. The boat was found, overturned, her husband's body carried to shore by the tides. Jacob's was never found. There was little doubt he had drowned. The fact that she had no grave to decorate changed nothing.

Her loss and grieving had cheated her baby out of the joys she should have known. Cat had been twelve when she remarried with the idea of a father for her. Irving hadn't turned out to be what she had hoped in a father or husband. Much older than she, she had nursed him through his illness, knowing all the time that she'd never really loved him.

She sucked in a breath pushing such memories from her. She would do what was required to find her daughter. She could not change the past. Perhaps she could the future. In the morning, she would try again to contact her detective to see what he knew.

She thought then about the man at the depot. The name Taggert had sounded familiar to her. Now she remembered why. The books she'd read had an outlaw hero by that name. Maybe a coincidence. Certainly, the man in the books had been younger than the one, who had delivered her to the hotel. The books were fiction anyway.

She called the desk to ask room service to bring her a meal-- even though she felt little like eating. She needed to eat, needed to get busy with finding Cat. She would endure whatever she must. She always did.

In the morning, Frederica went down the stairs to the dining room for breakfast. She had managed her hair in a simple bun and dressed in a plain, gray suit with white blouse.

"Howdy, ma'am," the voice behind her was familiar. She turned to look up into the eyes of the man called Taggert.

"You regularly eat here?" she asked with some suspicion.

"Now and again." He held a cup of coffee in his hand. A plate was on the table behind him. Perhaps her mistrust had been too quickly aroused. "You're welcome to share my table." Perhaps it hadn't been. She'd met too many fortune hunters. This outlaw might be one of them.

"You never gave me your last name but the clerk here knew it. Was there a reason?" she asked not answering his question.

"You don't like Jeremiah?" His smile was crooked and way too confident.

"But it's not all is it and often when someone avoids giving a last name, there is a reason."

He laughed, rose, held out a chair for her as though daring her to refuse. When the waitress came to take her order, she topped off his cup as well as filled one for her and handed her a menu.

"You look upset," he said with that smile that gave her a mixture of annoyance and attraction. "You know, you don't have to eat with me."

"Of course, I know that." She looked up at the waitress. "I'd like toast and two slices of bacon please."

"Sure thing, ma'am." With that, she was gone.

She looked back at Taggert, meeting his dark gaze and curious about who he was more than she wanted to admit. "Don't wait on finishing your meal for me," she said in what she thought was a polite tone.

His smile widened. He took a sip of his coffee. "Now about my name," he said, "it's known, is why I didn't mention it. Although I expect a lady like yourself, you'd never have heard it."

"As it happens I have. You are part of an outlaw family."

"Fictional."

Something about the way he said that sounded ironic. "Was it? The stories seemed pretty real."

"Good writer."

"The hero was an outlaw. Taggert without a first name. Might it have been Jeremiah?"

"Might but wasn't. I got to say I am surprised a lady like you would be reading dime novels."

She felt a little insulted. "Why not? I wanted to know what to expect out here. Even though I thought the West was tamed, I felt I should get different opinions."

He chuckled. "Dime novels won't do that for you. As it turns out though, the author happens to be my daughter-in-law."

"Wait, the author is a man. Will Tremaine."

"Authors use pseudonyms."

"Oh."

"Her husband isn't the man in her stories. Willy didn't even know him when she wrote them. Creative license, I believe they call it."

"Seems weirdly coincidental that they'd meet and then fall in love."

"Guess it would." He hesitated, and she wondered if he was going to say more as her toast and bacon strips arrived.

"Not much of a breakfast," he observed, as he got back to eating his own, which involved pancakes, eggs and sausages.

"So, no truth in the stories," she said as she sat back with her third cup of coffee.

"I didn't say that." He smiled again. "But not Cole, Vince or Jesse."

"And they would be?"

"My sons. Speaking of which, he looked up as a tall man entered the dining room. "This is one of them." He waved him to the table. The man's features, coloring and height would have made their relationship evident. "Mrs. Windsor, this is my son Vince Taggert." He smiled again. "Mrs. Windsor has come to Tucson on a mysterious mission."

"I did not say that," she corrected him.

He chuckled. "Nope."

"Happy to meet you, Mrs. Windsor," Vince said as she put out her hand, and he took it. His skin was rough, the kind a man got from working with his muscles. He turned back to his father. "I opened the shipment, and it wasn't what we had ordered."

"Excuse us, ma'am," Jeremiah rose and walked out to the lobby with his son.

So, he had not come to meet her, and it was another coincidence. She wasn't sure if she was disappointed. She didn't recall the last time she'd found a man attractive, but Jeremiah Taggert definitely was-- in a rugged, sort of dangerous way. Her husbands had both been gentle looking men. This man's face would never be considered gentle. Something though about him drew her in a peculiar way.

She shook her head. Ridiculous. She'd doubtless never see him again. The problem she had was whether she would see Cat. If her daughter wasn't here, where might she have gone? Fine detective she had hired when he couldn't give her an address or phone number where she could reach her daughter. Tucson was not a big city, but clearly also wasn't going to be an easy city to find one woman—especially if she didn't want to be found. Her main hope was that Cat had come to visit a friend. She had tried to telephone Grace Cordova, who had been a friend from university. They apparently had no phone. Was it even Grace, Cat had come to see?

When the waitress returned to refill her coffee cup, she raised her hand to stop her. "I was trying to reach Grace Cordova, would you happen to know her?"

The waitress considered a moment. "Yes, I do. Not like a friend or anything but everybody knows the Cordovas."

"Would you know where I could find her? She didn't appear to have a phone."

She saw the woman considering whether she wanted to tell her. "She lives at the Circle C, and no phones out there anyway."

"You know Grace?", Taggert asked as he returned and sat down to study her. He put his hand over his cup to signal no more coffee and the girl left them.

"She is or was a friend of my daughter's." She fought back tears. She would not show such weakness in a public place. Ladies did not do that.

He sipped his coffee giving her time. "So, you are actually here to meet your daughter."

She nodded, taking a lace trimmed handkerchief from her pocket and dabbing at her eyes. "In a way, but Cat is not expecting me. I hired a detective to find where my daughter went when she left Boston. He found she got as far as Tucson but then seemed to disappear. He found no address or way to contact her. He didn't think she had gone on though… when last he wired me."

"Not much of a detective."

"Apparently."

"I had a feeling you had a problem."

"Catherine left without telling me where she was going or why."

"She's a grown woman?"

"Twenty-eight."

"Then why not let her be?"

"Something about how she left made me uneasy. I was afraid she was in trouble. I worried that…" She didn't know why she would tell him so much, but she'd gone too far to quit. "I was concerned she was angry with me."

"And she hasn't contacted you?"

"No." She sniffled and felt angry as she again dabbed at her eyes with the handkerchief. "I'm afraid for her."

"You have a reason for that."

"Before she left Boston, she'd been avoiding me. It wasn't like her." She wouldn't tell him everything about Cat. She didn't know him well enough for that. Her whole escapade was beginning to seem foolish. She should have stayed in her home and hired a better detective.

"Tell me her name, and I'll see what I can do. Cole is a detective. He tends to be good at finding those who don't want to be found. One thing first though."

"Yes?"

"Is she in trouble with the law? If she is, Cole would turn her in."

"No, I am sure it's not that kind of trouble." She realized she wasn't totally confident as she looked up into his dark eyes. Could she trust this stranger? Did she have a choice? She had no idea how to proceed and no one to help her. She knew Cat was in trouble, the thought that she could not help her was painful.

CHAPTER 2

"I'd like to help you Mrs. Windsor, but you aren't giving me much to go on,"

"I'm sorry." From a woman who used to feel she knew how to take care of things, she'd gone to a confused muddle on the verge of tears.

"At least tell me her name and what she looks like."

"Catherine Lawrence. She looks a lot like me for features, size and height, but younger, of course. Her hair is red like her father's had been."

She saw him consider that. "Okay, finish your breakfast and then come with me," he said. "I have a friend who might be able to help you."

He quickly finished his own meal. She had to make herself eat her bacon and half a piece of toast. She had no appetite.

Outside, he helped her into his buggy.

"Your son doesn't need your assistance with whatever was wrong with that shipment?"

"Vince can take care of it." He lightly flicked the reins and drove into what now was some traffic on the street. "Busy season right before Christmas," he said. She saw more decorations on store windows, but the cactus made it look nothing like any Christmas she'd ever experienced.

"Is that a palm tree?" she asked.

"Some have been brought in, but that's a Joshua tree."

He pulled the buggy to a halt before a storefront. "Sicillas might know about your gal." Again, he helped her from the buggy. She liked the feel of his rough hand, and although she felt quite capable of alighting without assistance, she had waited.

Inside the store was filled with merchandise and shoppers. "Maybe this is a bad time," she said.

"Connie," he called to a red-haired woman who was behind the counter.

"Waiting for the last minute for Christmas shopping again?" the woman asked with a teasing smile.

"Nah, got that done. This lady though needs help. Her daughter came to Tucson, but she isn't sure where she landed, or even if she's still here. Mrs. Windsor, this is Mrs. Sicilla."

"Call me Connie. Your daughter's name is?"

Frederica repeated what she'd told him about the detective, and her hope that Grace Cordova would know where she was or maybe she'd be staying with her. "She would have arrived just under three months ago."

"And she intended to stay with Grace?"

"I don't even know for sure she went to Grace. I just assumed it when the detective said she had come to Tucson, and I remembered she and Grace went to college together. I've been foolish to come out here without knowing more."

"Come on back for a cup of tea, where we can talk more freely," Connie said. She looked then at Taggert, who was watching them with a contemplative expression. "Would you like some too, Jeremiah?"

He chuckled. "Thanks but nah. I will take a look at the rifles, seems like Del said he had a new one in that I'd want."

A male clerk came over. "Or that's an excuse and you want something stronger than tea."

"Hey, it's morning." She liked Taggert's laugh. It felt real, deep and resonating as though he saw humor in things others did not. She needed more humor—and that had been for a long, long time.

"Like that's ever stopped you before."

"You got anything better than the rotgut you tried to shove into me last time?"

"Come on over to the rifles and see." The clerk chuckled as the two headed to the other side of a store that clearly had womanly interests on one side and masculine on the other.

Connie directed Frederica to a door leading into a cozy kitchen. "Del is my husband. He has a bit of a sense of humor or so he thinks."

Frederica sat at a long table and managed a smile. Actually, a shot of whiskey sounded good to her too—morning or not. "Please call me Frederica." The kitchen had tall cupboards, and gingham curtains. It was more warm and inviting than her own kitchen in Boston—not that she spent much time there.

Connie poured hot water into a porcelain pot and brought it to the table, along with two cups. She sat across from Frederica. "Tell me now why you are concerned about your daughter."

"It wasn't like her to leave without saying where she was going. I came to believe someone was harassing her."

"A suitor?"

"I don't know for sure. Cat is a witch, Connie." She expected a look of shock, but Connie only nodded with an understanding expression. "She was running into problems in Boston from the things she had told others where it made them… afraid of her."

"Is she a natural born witch?"

She nodded. "A clairvoyant with certain powers. It has run in the family, but skipped me. My mother had it."

"Was your daughter prepared for what she knew and others did not?"

"I suppose I didn't do a good job with that. I lost my first husband and son when Cat was a baby."

"I'm so sorry."

Frederica sighed. "It was what it was. The thing was I lost track of what I still had. I grieved and then married a man, who I thought would be a father to Cat except he soon needed nursing care. I let down my daughter on so many counts."

"Those things do happen."

"I blame myself for not getting past it. Business became over-whelming with all I had to learn. My second husband had owned a shipping business, which I inherited. Actually, both my husbands were wealthy. It ended up being a lot of responsibility to manage the businesses. There were employees and…" She felt annoyed at how defensive she sounded. She had done what she had to do. She shook her head and met Connie's sympathetic gaze. "You are a stranger. I have told you too much."

Connie smiled. "You need some help to work through all of this. If I can help, I am glad to."

"The thing is I realize now that Cat needed more from me than I gave her. She became secretive, avoided telling me about her life."

"She was living home when she left for Tucson?"

"No, she was working. Cat is a talented decorator and designer. She had wanted her own home. I understood that and helped her economically to set up her business. She didn't seem to want a husband, and I accepted that too-- given the pain mine had caused me. I thought she could take care of everything."

"Do you have a reason for believing she is not?"

"Why Tucson, and why not tell me where she was going or even that she was? When I realized she had closed up her business and home, I made inquiries, and it's when I hired the detective... for all the good he's done me. I don't know that she is even here. She may have gotten back on the train and headed on."

"Other friends?"

"She had friends in San Francisco too." She felt the tears at her feeling of total helplessness. If something happened to her daughter, she'd never forgive herself.

"All right," Connie said rising from the table. "Drink your tea, and let me see what I can find out. I don't see Grace often with the babies and the ranch. Unfortunately, the Circle C does not have phone service. Let me see what their friends and family here know."

"I am sorry to trouble you."

"It's no problem."

Federica sat sipping her tea, feeling lost, as Connie made one call and then another. She knew it would not be good news when Connie sat back down. "I tried Rafe's parents. No answer, which is not a surprise. Maria cleans homes, and Raul works for various ranchers. I thought Ollie and Rose might know about Grace and Rafe, but again no answer. They might also have gone down to the O'Brian ranch on the border, which might also be where Grace and her family have gone."

"For what?"

"Christmas. I believe I had heard the Rykers would also be there—they all make a big thing out of Christmas."

"I understand." She didn't. She'd never known a family Christmas. Her birth family had been more into wealth than love. Decorations were to be admired, not touched. Gifts were lavish but with little real caring behind them. She had no one but herself to blame for how she handled her own family. She fought back the tears. "I am sorry to have troubled you."

"I just regret that I don't have more to tell you. You mentioned a detective."

"Lot of good he has done me but yes."

"Perhaps you should contact him."

"I guess I will have to. Thank you, Connie."

"If I get anything or hear more, I will contact you. Where are you staying?"

"The Santa Rita. I appreciate your trying."

Back in the store, she wondered if Jeremiah had waited for her and then saw him leaning against a counter and talking to Connie's husband. One booted foot was crossed over the other, with his arms folded across his chest. She felt an odd throb in her heart. Maybe she'd felt that before, but it had been too many years to be sure.

He walked to her. "Find out anything?"

She shook her head. "I will have to wait to find out if Cordovas had seen Cat. If she was with them or…" She felt lost. Wilson would be in Tucson in a few days maybe. He had no reason to think she needed him, and she didn't want to ruin his time with his family.

Outside, he helped her into his buggy. "Connie couldn't help you?" he asked.

"She tried, but it appears no one was home who might know."

"Tell me more about the situation."

His tone demanded she level with him, and she told him all she knew, including the witch part. She had glanced over when she said it, but he showed no reaction.

"Tell me the name of your detective."

"Why? He hasn't bothered to contact me since he told me she was in Tucson."

"Might be you need to know more about him." He flicked the reins and started the buggy back toward her hotel.

"What do you mean?"

"Not everyone who says they are a detective is. Name?"

"Bryce McClure."

"Eastern fella?"

"He worked out of an office in Boston."

"And he came out here to trace her down?"

She felt like a total fool. "I don't know." She sucked in a breath trying to stop the tears that wanted to come. "He gave me a report, and I paid him."

"Most folks aren't good at working with detectives, and there are crooks taking advantage of that." He gave a little laugh, but when she looked over at him, again she could not read his face.

"The first thing you need to know is if she's in Tucson. I will set Cole on finding out about your detective, checking rentals in town, whether he was ever here, but for now, why don't we take a little ride out to the Cordova spread?"

"We could do that?" She was out of her depths.

"Sure. Won't take that long. If they are gone, the hands will know where. If they're there, they may know where your daughter is."

She felt close to tears again. And then she thought of something deeper, more primal as a concern, why should she trust this man? He might take her out onto the desert and kill her.

"So, what's it to be?" he asked pulling the horses to a halt. "Back to your hotel or the Circle C?"

She had little to lose. "How long would it take?"

"Forty-five minutes, maybe more. Faster on horseback. You ride?"

"Some." She wasn't about to tell him all her own secrets.

"You know, sometimes just being out on the desert helps clear a body's mind." When she didn't immediately answer, he said, "I can take you to the livery and have Hank drive you out if you don't trust me."

She heard no resentment in his voice. It seemed going out there was her only way to find out if Cat was there, or if they had seen her. It was tempting on more than one count. She had seen the mountains ringing Tucson, but had only seen the countryside from the train—something about the desert was intriguing her. "Please, yes, if it's not too much trouble."

"You didn't eat enough to keep a bird alive for breakfast. How about I buy you lunch, and then we head out there."

"Except I pay," she said. "I insist as you are providing me a service."

His smile was crooked. "Sure, you pay if you want." He stopped the buggy in front of a small café. Soon they were inside and had ordered sandwiches from the attractive but older waitress.

"This is Laura," Jeremiah said when she brought them their sandwiches. "Laura, this is Mrs. Windsor."

"Frederica, please," she said, as she bit into the sandwich with real hunger that surprised her. By her second cup of coffee, she realized she had another need.

"You want to wash up," Jeremiah said, "the lavatory is through that door."

She smiled with relief. Returning, found him chatting with the waitress. Maybe they were more than friends. Laura was attractive enough to interest a man. She judged her to be around her age.

"I better hit it too," Jeremiah said with a grin, and disappeared through the door.

"Want a refill of your coffee?" Laura asked.

"I better not. The roast beef sandwich was very good. Horseradish on it, wasn't it?"

"It was. Most around here like things spicy. I hope it wasn't too much for you."

"No, it was delicious."

When Jeremiah returned, he didn't protest when she paid, leaving a generous tip. Outside, he said, "Generally I like to do the paying."

"Is that a rule?" she asked as he helped her into the buggy.

When he came around to his side, he said, "It would be if I wasn't taking you somewhere and providing a service." His tone was cryptic.

She had second thoughts of the wisdom of this, as he turned them first north and then east. In half an hour, the road was lined with tall saguaros. Boulders seemed to have been put in place just to enhance the beauty.

"Have you lived here long, Mr. Taggert?" she asked, as she broke a silence that was making her uneasy.

"Not very. I lived in Utah for more years. Born in Kansas." He glanced over at her. "Mrs. Windsor, you don't have to go out here with me. We can turn around right now, if you feel uncomfortable about being alone with me."

She swallowed, one of her hands holding on the rail at the side of the buggy, the other resting on her lap was in a fist. She tried to relax. "You do rather look like an outlaw."

His laugh was deep. He turned the buggy around.

"No, don't, please. I want to go out. I know those book covers don't really show what outlaws are like."

"Sometimes they are pretty close." His tone was dry. "But you are safe with me. It's up to you whether we turn back."

She contemplated that. "Please take me out to the ranch. I need to know where Cat is. I have no reason to distrust you."

He turned the buggy. With a flick of the reins, they were again heading up the road. He drove smoothly, moving to the edge as they passed wagons and riders coming into town. The most unusual sights for her were the men with small horses and little wagons or sometimes bearing bundles of wood.

"Those horses are certainly small," she said with an attempt at normalizing conversation between them.

"Donkeys. See the long ears. Not horses."

She felt embarrassed again. She knew so little about the world beyond ships, offices and books full of numbers.

"I can see how this is different for you, strange place."

"It is that."

"Especially after reading those Taggert books." He glanced over and then back at the road.

"Of course, I realize they were all made up." She knew she was trying to reassure herself.

"Don't want to scare you, ma'am."

"Frederica."

He smiled at that. "There was some truth in them, or they'd not have been so popular."

She wasn't sure she wanted to know how much truth.

"The Taggert family did have their share and then some of scalawags."

"Scalawags?" This was a foreign language as well as a strange land.

"Men who rode the other side of the law." He stared toward the hills. "I'll tell you about it sometime, but now we have to turn off and this road takes a little more care to not break a wheel."

Surprising to her, she felt no fear at what he'd said. She settled back to enjoy the desert terrain as the cactus were more profuse with varieties she'd never seen. Sometimes, Jeremiah pointed to one and told her its name. The strangest were the ocotillo with long spiny arms rising from the desert floor, almost looking dead.

He pointed to the left. "See the coyote." It ran in a zigzag pattern and soon disappeared.

"Are they dangerous?"

"To rabbits and sheep, if anybody was fool enough to bring them here, goats sometimes."

"They look like wolves."

"Small ones."

Another mile, had her seeing her first deer, before it bounded away. When the strangest bird that she'd ever seen, ran across the track chasing a lizard, he said, "Road runner."

"So much wildlife out here."

"Rafe and Grace are good at handling their land. They don't over-graze. They protect the springs and creeks. In a desert like this, it's what keeps a ranch going, to know enough to do that." He pointed then, and she saw the buildings nestled against a bluff. Five minutes later, they were in the yard. He helped her down from the buggy. "Since they didn't come out, my guess is they are gone. Let me find a hand."

He left her by the front porch of a sprawling home, made of what looked like the earth. The tile roof was red. Flowers bloomed around the posts of the porch. When he returned, a dark skinned handsome man was with him. "Mrs. Windsor, this is Gabe Cordova, Rafe's brother. He's looking after the place along with two hands, who are out right now. The family went to the Circle O, and your daughter is with them."

She felt a wave of relief. "Will they return after Christmas?" she asked.

Gabe shook his head. "After New Year's. It's a big celebration down there."

That was a disappointment, but her relief outweighed it. "Thank you so much," she said.

"You being Cat's mother," Gabe said, "you are welcome to stay here until they return."

She shook her head. She would be better off at the hotel. "Thank you though," she said.

"Would you like lemonade before you head back?" Gabe asked.

Jeremiah studied the sky. "No, I want her back before dark." His gaze met hers. "Do you want some water before we head out?"

"I'm fine."

In moments, they were back on the road.

"Should I hire someone to take me to her?" she mused out loud.

"You could but that's rugged country, two nights camping to get to the ranch. Unless you know something more than you've said, why not wait for her to come back."

"You're right, of course. At least I know she's with someone she cares for and is safe."

The sun was moving toward the western mountains as they drove into town. In front of the hotel, he pulled the team to a halt. "I will find out about your detective," he said.

"Thank you but I am less concerned than I was. Knowing she is with family for Christmas makes me feel better, and I can wait to see her." It would be a lonely Christmas for her, but she'd had those before. At least, this one would not be one of grieving. When she saw Cat, she'd find out why she'd cut her from her life.

"Before you go in," he said, "I should tell you something."

"All right."

"Are you familiar with Quantrill's Raiders?"

The name sounded familiar. "The Civil War?"

"Yes, I rode with them."

"What were they exactly?"

"Pro-Confederate rangers, more commonly called bushwhackers. We fought like Apaches. Bill Quantrill led us. During those years, I met a lot of names you probably know like Jesse James."

She felt her face whiten. "Yes… I recognize the name."

"In the beginning of the war, Kansas and Missouri were supposed to be Union, but it was really bandit country. There was a lot of fighting over territory. Kansas was bloody ground. A man learned to fight in ways that kept him alive, but can't say proud of how it was. It fit a man like me."

"What do you mean by that?"

"Remember those books you read?"

"Yes. You said they were fictional."

"Part of them. The Taggerts were outlaws, before the War. My father, Josiah was good at robbing, an murderin'. His brother, Jericho, during a disagreement, killed him. It's likely that Pa wasn't mentally right and that led to his end. Maybe none of the brothers were right in the head. They were outlaws, and it was reading about them, that triggered Willy to write the first of her books, making up what she hadn't read."

"Oh my."

"Mrs. Windsor, you weren't wrong when you labeled me an outlaw. I was one for a lot of years. It was a way of life in Kansas and later."

She tried to take it in. "And your sons' mother? Your mother?"

"My mother died of a broken heart most likely. Yolinda was a good woman. She didn't like what was going on. It's not much of a life for women to have their men on the outlaw trail. I was married twice and both my wives died. Agatha before the war. She was quite a woman, rode a horse better than a man. When she got pregnant, it never occurred to either of us that she would die in it, but she did. Vince survived. There was a neighbor girl, looked with favor on me. I needed a mother for Vince and married Valerie same year. She was more fragile than I knew. Her soul took a battering by what was going on, by how we had to live. She kept begging me to leave Kansas. The war meant I couldn't. I wasn't there much for her. Then the war was over. She begged me to leave, give up the scavenging, killing, fighting. She said I'd end up dead or in prison. My uncles didn't see it that way, but I packed up what I could in a wagon, took the horses I owned, with Vince riding one of them even at five, and we set out. Her, with Asa in her arms, and we headed for Utah where we bought a hardscrabble ranch."

She stared at the hotel door, wondering if she needed to get out of this buggy, whether she wanted to hear more. She had heard the pain in Jeremiah's voice. "When you got there, did you stop... what you knew to do?" she asked finally.

He sucked in a breath. "You mind if I smoke?"

"It's not very good for you."

He smiled at that. "A lot of things ain't." He pulled a cigarette from his pocket and struck a match on his boot. Lighting the cigarette, he took a long draw and let out the smoke.

"So, no I didn't stop what I knew as a way to make a living. Those were wild times. Bank robberies, robbing trains for a while, worked as a way to make a living. The ranch wasn't on good land for cattle. Valerie got colder toward me, and I couldn't blame her.

She nagged that it was wrong, even as we had two more boys, Cole and then Jesse. Jesse wasn't quite right in the head, something about his birth or the damned family... pardon my language."

She felt herself grinding her teeth and tried to relax. "Were your boys outlaws too then?"

"Only Asa. He took to the life. Vince hated it, didn't like Asa's bullying and took off when he was not more than a kid. I guess Valerie helped him get away. I chased after him, didn't want to lose my boy, but it took years to cross his trail. When I saw he was all right, I had to let it go. Likely, he was better off away from us."

"You are telling me a tragic story of loss, crime, and violence. It's hard for me to grasp." She wondered why he wanted her to know such sordid details of his life. "You said your second wife also died?"

He drew on the cigarette. "She was murdered."

She felt her face whiten as the shock went through her. "How did..."

"I only learned the why of it years later. At the time, all I knew was she was sick and got sicker. Doc couldn't figure out what was wrong. It was years later after coming to Tucson when it finally came out and Jesse told me. Asa had bragged to him about it after he'd done it. Jesse had kept the secret because his mama was dead. He saw no point in telling anyone. He had and still has a simple, earthy way of thinking."

"I'm trying to get my head around this. Your son murdered his own mother?"

He let out a cloud of smoke. "He had all the bad of the Taggerts. Anyway, he's dead now too."

"I don't know what to say."

"I am not asking for absolution, Mrs. Windsor. I just wanted you to know your instincts that first day weren't wrong." He threw the cigarette into the street, jumped down and ground it out with his boot before he came around to help her down.

"You didn't need to tell me," she said as they walked up the steps to the hotel.

"Yes, I did." He looked down at her when they reached the door. "I, most especially, needed you to know." With that, he was gone.

CHAPTER 3

J eremiah took the buggy back to the livery. "You look fit to be tied," Hank said as Jeremiah began unhitching his team.

"I've had better days," Angry with himself and the world, he freed his geldings into one corral and retrieved his bay, Blasted, from another.

"You want me to keep these two or you coming for them?" Hank pointed to his team.

"For a few days. I have something I need to take care of." He threw the saddle over his bay, rubbing Blasted's neck as he added the hackamore. Stepping into the saddle, he lightly nudged the gelding's side to encourage a faster pace as he headed north-- in the mood to tear something apart.

As he rode, he felt angry with himself for the emotions surging through him. It was his own fault. He had brought all this on himself, and it wasn't the only time. He wished he hadn't agreed to do Vince a favor and picking up those boxes. He wished he hadn't noticed her standing alone, looking lost-- so beautiful, such a classy lady, and the last woman he ever should know. He had put himself beyond the pale so many years ago that he barely even knew when it all went wrong.

When he was away from the houses, he urged his gelding to a gallop, hoping he could work some of his frustration out. When he got to the turn off for Ollie Oliver's desert home, he took it, unsure why. Maybe he wanted someone else to beat up on him. Maybe he'd be lucky, and Ollie, Rose, and their grandson, Royce would be gone south to the Circle O. He wasn't sure he wanted to talk to anyone, or maybe he did, and it's why he'd turned right rather than continuing on out to Oracle.

At the Oliver hacienda, he saw horses in the corral. Before he dismounted, Ollie came out of the house. "Whatcha been up to?" his old friend asked.

"I thought you'd be gone," he said dismounting and tying Blasted's reins to the hitching post.

"So ya come up here to rob us?" Ollie asked with a chuckle.

"Exactly. Got anything worth robbing?"

"Might have some Jack Daniels." Ollie laughed again. "Is it too early?"

"Never too early." Jeremiah dropped into one of the chairs on the veranda, taking the shot glass when Ollie handled it to him. The two old friends sipped in silence as Jeremiah tried to think whether he really wanted to tell Ollie anything. "Where are Rose and Royce?"

"Should be back from town soon. Royce has had a cold that hung on, a hackin' cough. She took him to see Doc."

Jeremiah frowned and let out a breath. He well understood how those things could escalate. "Hope he'll be okay. Is that why you didn't head south with Cordovas?"

"One of them. What's up with you? You look sourer than a pickle."

Jeremiah lit a cigarette staring into the distance. The Oliver home nestled into the desert but beyond the valley laid out, as far as the distant Tucson Mountains. "You know a Bryce McClure?" he asked finally.

Ollie considered that. "Is there a reason I should?"

"He might've come here. He is supposed to be a detective looking for a woman, who was a friend of Grace's."

"Cat?"

"You met her?"

"Sure did. Lovely woman. Red hair. Who forgets red hair."

"How about McClure, did you meet him?"

"Describe him. The name doesn't ring a bell."

"I never saw him. I should have asked."

"Asked?"

Jeremiah took a long draw on his cigarette. Cat's mother is here in Tucson to find her. She hired a detective who told her that she'd come here but then no more information."

Ollie shook his head. "That doesn't sound good."

"Yeah."

"You want to call Cole from here?"

"Your line working?"

Ollie gave him a look. "You know how to hurt a man."

Jeremiah grinned. "Then yes, I would like to use your phone." They went into the kitchen and he picked up the receiver, not happy to be doing this. He had a feeling it would ensnare him more than he already was. Still, he had promised he'd try to find out what he could. When Willy answered, he asked if Cole was nearby.

"He's at the barn. Want me to get him?"

He considered that. "I can ride down if you'll be there." He felt like taking Blasted for a long, hard gallop. Luckily, his big bay was up to just that and would enjoy it as much as he would.

"Have dinner with us," she said as she hung up.

"What the hell is this about?" Ollie asked.

"I'm trying to do a favor for a lady. That's all."

"And it's got you by the tail and swinging you into something I ain't never seen. Explain that?"

"You are a nosy old man."

Ollie smirked. "You wanted to tell me. So, do it."

"It's the mother."

Ollie let out a whistle. "Look anything like her daughter?"

"Haven't seen the daughter, but Mrs. Windsor is beautiful, kind of aged some but like a fine wine." He managed a smile that he didn't feel.

"My God, I never heard you talk like that. You're attracted to her." It wasn't a question.

"No." He didn't want to be, so he wouldn't be. She was out of his league in a hundred ways. Since Valerie had died, the only women he'd been with were whores and not that many of those. He had thought that part of his life was over, and it was.

"Something wrong with her?"

"With me." He smiled. He'd get past this.

"I don't see anything wrong with you."

Jeremiah laughed, took a long draw on his cigarette, and rose. "I need to get going."

"Come back when you want to talk."

"Good luck with your grandson." He patted Ollie's shoulder, stepped off the porch. At the corral, he threw down his cigarette, ground it out with his boot, and stepped into the saddle. He turned Blasted down the road, knowing Ollie was watching him.

As he rode back down the road, he didn't know why he had come, except Ollie was a good man and his best friend. Something about the old-timer, maybe his own outlaw past, gave the two a connection that Jeremiah welcomed. It had been rare in his life. Mostly, when a man rode the outlaw trail, he learned to trust few men or women. A man lived longer that way. Since he'd changed his ways, something he hadn't done willingly, he had resisted making friends just out of habit. Ollie had gotten in before he'd been aware what was happening.

Riding into the Taggert ranch grounds, he saw his son coming out of the barn and waving. Cole was tall, dark-haired, looked a lot like his brothers—well, Jesse was bigger than the rest but other than that, they looked like matched sets. He felt proud of the men they'd become and gave himself no credit for that. Asa was his fault. Jesse, Cole and Vince all went to Valerie's credit or maybe just their own natures.

"What's up, Pa?" Cole asked as soon as Jeremiah stepped from the saddle.

"I need your help to find out if a Bryce McClure came to Tucson, whether he's a detective or even more so if he's a man to be trusted." He told Cole the bare facts of Mrs. Windsor's journey to find her daughter and her concerns as to the reasons she'd left Boston.

"Off hand, the name doesn't ring a bell. Let me call Jace and see what he knows. You staying for supper?"

"Willy asked me but not sure." Much as he was proud of his sons, they also reminded him of a part of his life he preferred not to remember.

"Well, let's put your horse in the corral and come on in and I'll see what I can find out."

In the house, Cole's beautiful bride came out from the kitchen. "I was fixing a roast with potatoes. There is plenty. You are staying," Willy said with a grin as she watched Cole and Jeremiah unbuckle their gun belts and hang them on the hooks by the door.

"Do you two really need to wear guns all the time?" she asked with hands on her hips as the two men washed up. "Times have changed, and we're more civilized now, don't you think?"

Before Jeremiah could answer, Cole did. "I guess I could take my chances with one of my enemies showing up and count on you to talk him into leaving." He shot his wife a grin as he dried his hands.

She gave him one of her looks. "Arizona will be a state soon."

"Maybe," Jeremiah said. "In the meantime, there are still those who would shoot Taggerts in the back. Not saying they might not have reason." He grinned.

Willy let out a snort. "Don't they weigh you down?"

"The reason for them more than the guns," Jeremiah said with more introspection in his comment than he usually shared. "I agree there will come a day men don't need them," Jeremiah said. "It will be longer before it's men like my sons or me." He accepted the towel from his son and dried his own hands. He wished he could remove from them more than the water, maybe the memory of all they had done.

"What about staying for dinner?" she asked clearly giving up the argument, at least for the moment as they moved to the parlor.

"I reckon I am."

"I'll see what I can find out," Cole said heading back to the kitchen and the phone.

"Want a glass of wine?" Willy asked Jeremiah.

"Got something stronger," he asked cocking his head a little.

"Brandy?"

"Stronger?"

She laughed and went to the sideboard to pour a shot glass of whiskey. "We haven't seen much of you since the wedding." She sat across from him on the sofa.

He settled onto one of their overstuffed chairs. "It's only been two weeks," he said taking a sip of the good whiskey.

She laughed. "Seems longer."

"A lot has happened."

"It has." She hesitated. "Have you heard from Nate since he went back to Frisco?"

"Figure you would if anyone did."

"He seemed to be friends with you."

"But best friends with you. With me, it was just while he stayed in my place." Nate Hemstreet had probably gotten his fill of the west with the gunfight he'd taken part in as Willy's enemy came for her, and the Taggerts took care of it. That young man had been pretty pale afterward. Likely, he would avoid reminders of it. "You should write him if you're worried about him," Jeremiah said taking the remainder of the whiskey in a slug.

"Probably better as it is. I do worry though given his mother." Willy sighed.

"She's a corker all right. You been writing a new book? She might make a good villain for you."

She laughed. "She's probably not bad enough to be a good villain. I don't think Cole wants me writing more books. They've caused him trouble."

"You can't not do what's right for you, gal."

"I know but… I'd have to come up with a new hero. I am not fond of drawing danger to my man."

"Bet you could do that. By the way, I met a fan of your books."

"Another retired gunman?" she teased.

"A lady from Boston." He told her how he'd met Mrs. Windsor and why he'd come to ask Cole's help for her.

"My, that is something of a coincidence," she said.

"What's that mean?"

"Nothing." Her smile didn't look like nothing. He didn't want her getting any matchmaking ideas, but before he could set her straight, Cole came back into the parlor and poured himself a shot. "The name didn't register with Jace. If he came to Tucson, he didn't check in with the sheriff's office or so far as he knew not the marshal's either. However, he has a friend in the Boston police department, who will know about detectives working there at least, but it might take a while."

"Hopefully this is not a problem needing to be taken care of right away." The trouble was, he was getting that itch that told him something about this wasn't how Frederica Windsor thought it was.

"Will she be here through Christmas?" Willy asked.

"Until her daughter comes back with Grace, I guess."

"Then she is spending it with us." She smiled. "I must meet a woman, who is actually a fan of my books." She gave a little laugh when Cole gave her one of his looks, the ones Jeremiah had seen all too often from his son.

"Your wife's gonna write a new one," Jeremiah said.

"Happiness is. Who does Taggert kill this time?"

Jeremiah chuckled. "Gotta give them a happily ever after, don't ya?"

Cole let out a sigh. "When's dinner going to be ready?"

"Soon. Don't look so glum I haven't actually started writing anything. Your father was pulling your leg." She giggled.

"Should that phrase mean something to me?" Cole asked with a crooked grin.

"Came across it in research. It relates to criminals in England."

"And it means?"

"Well, basically fooling with someone. It came from when criminals in England would string a wire and it would trip their prey. When he fell, they'd grab his valuables."

"No guns for the victims, I take it," Jeremiah said with a chuckle.

She took a sanctimonious pose, which on such a beautiful woman made him grin. "Of course, not. England was civilized."

"Other than the criminals."

"Other than."

"Maybe you should base your next book there," Cole suggested.

"I think not. I like Western outlaws better." She rose and headed for the kitchen.

"You sure got lucky with that woman, son," Jeremiah said.

Cole shook his head. "Don't I know it. Pure luck is exactly what it was too. Now tell me more about this Mrs. Windsor besides that she likes Will Tremaine's books."

"I don't know much. Just came across her like I said, and she had a problem I thought you might be able to help her with."

"It's not all about finding her daughter, is it?"

Jeremiah rose and walked to the fireplace staring into its darkness. "Should build a fire," he said. "Even Tucson gets cold in December."

Cole laughed. "Tell me what's going on… when you're ready."

It was dark when Jeremiah rode back into Tucson, debating whether to head downtown or to his bungalow. In the end, the bungalow won because he had no idea what to say to her. He needed more information. The fact that his instincts told him that she was in more trouble than she knew, wouldn't impress her much, if he didn't have a reason—besides the itch that had saved his life more than once.

He rode Blasted into the small shed at the back of his home. He removed the saddle and hackamore, filled the wooden trough with hay, and curried his horse before he finally checked the water and headed for his back porch. It had been a long day.

The striped gray cat that had been hanging around meowed loudly as Jeremiah opened the kitchen door. "Still haven't found a home?" he asked the stray. He had been feeding it for a few months, and it appeared that left him the designated servant. He shook his head but stood aside to let the cat into the kitchen. "Not much here to eat," he said, thinking he probably needed to buy cat food. So far, it had been living on his leftovers. That could not be good for cats—especially not where he didn't always have that many leftovers.

"What's your name?" he asked turning on the electric light, as he found some leftover beef trimmings and put it in a plate for the cat to gobble up. He filled a small bowl with water and set it beside the plate. He poured a shot of whiskey as he thought about the problem of Mrs. Windsor and her daughter. What was it that was riding him about it?

The cat looked up at him with an inquisitive expression that might or not mean something. He'd never had a cat, not that many pets. "Plain gray color. Okay, you are Scamp. How's that suit you?" Since the cat didn't object, he felt it was as good as anything. He'd put a blanket into the corner by the stove and Scamp headed for it with a full belly. He'd been pretty scruffy looking when he'd first seen him on his porch but had put on weight. He didn't want a pet. He didn't want anything he had to take care of. His own life was not that guaranteed. Still, the cat needed someone, and no one else appeared to be taking on the job.

He sipped his whiskey as he thought about Mrs. Windsor and the little he knew about her. She had obviously trusted the detective she hired. How had she found the man? Had she researched him or trusted someone who had given her references? Had she thought to ask for references? Questions raced through his mind with no answers. None that even Mrs. Windsor was likely to know.

The ringing phone interrupted his musing. It was Cole.

"Jace got back to me sooner than I expected. You ready for the report?"

He listened for the telltale sign that someone was listening in. When he didn't hear it, he said, "Shoot."

"First, how did your friend find this *detective*?"

"Not legit?"

"Not close. He also has multiple aliases. In Boston, he's been on the shady side of everything. More damning, he generally works for Jonathan Cheshire—a man you apparently don't want to know or deal with. How would Mrs. Windsor have found her detective?"

"I don't know. Tell me more about Cheshire." He balanced the receiver on his shoulder as he lit a cigarette.

"Runs both sides of the street. He's got a polished side, lots of money, many fronts in what look like establishment businesses. It isn't how he makes his real fortune. He's a smuggler and crime boss. You pay him off if you want your business to do well, if you don't want it burned to the ground. Definitely not a man to cross. It's strange that his man ended up being her detective. I wonder if she knows Cheshire."

"She ran a shipping business. Seems possible." He took a long draw on his cigarette.

He heard Cole suck in a breath. "I suggest she fire the detective and make sure she has nothing more to do with Cheshire."

"Maybe she never did."

"Meaning?"

"For some reason, her daughter left Boston without telling her mother why. Maybe she's the one who ran afoul of Cheshire. How far do his tentacles run?" He'd certainly seen plenty on that level who reached across the country.

"But why would she?"

"She was running a decorating business. From what Ollie said, she's a beautiful woman. Maybe she ran across him and couldn't get shed of him."

"Wow, that could be. All right, what do we do?"

"We? I need information but don't want you involved, Cole. You just got married, plus are still healing from nearly getting killed. Thanks though for finding what I needed."

"What are you going to do?"

"Talk to Mrs. Windsor in the morning, and play it from there."

When he hung up, he considered what he could do. What he wanted to do was never see the woman again. He'd fallen in love twice, but nothing had felt like this. He wasn't sure what was drawing him to her so strongly, but strong as it was, even stronger was his fear. He couldn't take another heartbreak, and that was bound to happen. She was out of his league, would have been even if he'd not had a past that nothing was ever going to wipe clean.

Because of all he felt, he had to help her, but maybe he'd find a way to do it from a distance. First, he needed to know more about her or her daughter's connection to Jonathan Cheshire. He didn't need to know the man, to know the type. He needed to know how she found her detective. It's possible that she had more than one problem.

Waking at first light, Jeremiah fixed breakfast and fed Scamp who rewarded him by rubbing around his legs. He didn't want a cat. Why had he started feeding one? He knew the answer. In some ways, he admired the little animal, who had not had an easy time to survive but never gave up. He wondered if Scamp liked milk. The widow woman who lived two houses down from his had a cow. He might try to buy some from her. That wasn't smart. That lady had had her eye on him since he'd bought the bungalow.

Still, it might put some weight on Scamp, make his coat smoother.

Outside, he fed his horse, curried him again, with Scamp dogging his feet... if dogging was the right word for a cat. Back inside the cat beat him through the door. He guessed he'd have to rig up some kind of dirt box as he vaguely recalled cats would use such things. Maybe...

By nine, he felt he could risk calling the hotel to see if Mrs. Windsor was up yet.

"And who is asking?"

"Taggert."

He heard the momentary hesitation. "She's in the dining room," the clerk said finally. "Would you like me to deliver a message to her?"

"Yes, when she has time, ask her to call Taggert." He gave him the number. "Tell her I have some information for her."

"Yes sir."

He was smoking his third cigarette of the morning when the phone rang.

"We need to talk," he said after the polite hellos.

"Can't you tell me what you learned over the phone."

"Best not. Some lines have more listeners than others." He smiled as he heard the click of the clerk hanging up.

"All right. When?"

"There is a little park near the hotel. Can you be there in fifteen minutes?"

"Yes."

"Wear a coat. It's a little cool out."

"All right."

Saddling Blasted, he put aside his doubts at seeing her again. The mystery of what was going on tweaked his curiosity. More than that, his itch was getting stronger. He needed to take care of that. He just hoped he was overreacting and there was nothing to be concerned about. He had put on his gun belt, even after Willy's chiding. He imagined Mrs. Windsor didn't think too much of wearing guns though she'd said little about it. A lot of men could quit wearing guns, didn't need them. He wasn't one of them.

CHAPTER 4

Frederica had taken his advice and worn a long tan jacket. She had coiled her dark hair at the nape of her neck. The park he had suggested was a short walk from the hotel. The trees were tall, still leafy, which didn't seem right for it being nearly Christmas. Someone had put glass ornaments on one of the trees and tied red and green bows on the park bench. She studied the colorful painting on a nearby wall. The images depicted a family with Tucson buildings and the desert in the background. Very nice, a bit like a painter, whose work she admired, Paul Gauguin.

She was still a little amazed to see flowers blooming in the middle of winter. The breeze carried a slightly lemony scent, but she couldn't find its source. When she heard the sound of hooves, a horse coming fast, she turned to watch Taggert ride up, jump from his saddle and tie the horse's reins to a post before coming to her.

"We should sit a spell," he suggested pointing to the bench.

When they were sitting, a few inches between them, he said, "I need more information."

She nodded.

"How did you find McClure?"

"My majordomo, Wilson, found him and brought him to my home for an interview and then instructions. He came highly recommended."

"By who?"

"Tell me first why this matters."

"McClure is a shady operator with more than one name. He mostly works for a man named Jonathan Cheshire. Do you know him?"

She hadn't expected that. "I've met him at parties, events, of course, but I can't say I know him. How could McClure work for him though? He's a detective with an office."

"You visited it?"

"Well, no. Wilson did that for me."

"What's the rest of Wilson's name?"

"You are asking a lot more questions than giving me answers." She felt a shiver of fear as she saw the sternness in his narrowed eyes.

"I need the answers to help you. When I know who Wilson is, I can find out more about him."

"Isn't it enough that I know him. He's worked for my second husband when I married him. And he helped us immensely when my husband grew ill. After William died, he was there for me."

"And his name is." He lit a cigarette.

"Wilson Potter. He's very efficient, caring, and I know he's honorable."

Taggert took a long drag on his cigarette. "Mrs. Windsor, you need to understand something. Often people come on one way to get something."

She felt annoyed. "Of course, I know that."

"Do you?" He met her gaze directly. "Would this Wilson know all you know about Catherine?"

"You mean her friend here. Of course."

"Why didn't he come to Tucson with you?"

"He'll be here in a day or two. He had family in El Paso. I insisted he spend time with them." She suddenly wondered if that was so. Whose idea had it been for him not to come with her? She pressed her lips together. "I've known him for a long time and you hardly at all. You admitted you were an outlaw. Why should I trust you about any of this?"

He shrugged taking another long draw on his cigarette before blowing the smoke away from her. "It's up to you."

She had to think about that. For some reason, she did trust him. It seemed foolish but. "All right," she said. "I have to trust you."

He smiled at that as he rose. "I need to call Cole and see what he can find out about Potter. He has a source in Boston. I am concerned right now for your daughter and you."

"You are frightening me," she said standing and looking up into his eyes.

"Fear can be a good thing sometimes." His expression was so steely. She had to remember that he had faced down things and lived to be this old. He probably did have good instincts.

"I will try to keep it under control," she said.

He smiled. "I'll meet you at Sicillas in say an hour. Can you do that?"

"Why there?"

"I trust them, and Connie can help you with the fear as well as provide good insights—if she so chooses."

"All right."

He rode off and she watched until he disappeared around a corner. She walked slowly back to her hotel as she considered his words about what she had thought she knew. Now she wondered if she knew any of it.

"Mrs. Windsor," the clerk said when she entered the hotel. "You have a message."

She looked at the words on the paper trying to get her head around them. Wilson would arrive on the evening train. She let out a breath. This didn't appear to be good timing. She wanted more time to assimilate what she'd been told—little though it was.

An hour later, she walked into Sicillas' store, disappointed that Taggert was not already there.

"Good to see you again," Connie said coming to her. "Can I help you with anything?"

"I was supposed to meet Jeremiah Taggert here. I hope you don't mind if I wait."

"Would you like a cup of tea while you wait?"

Frederica smiled. "I always love a cup of tea." Once again in the cozy kitchen, she though how she envied Connie on many levels. Not so much money probably, but she clearly had a purpose, a loving husband, and seemed comfortable with who she was. In some ways, Frederica didn't think she ever had had that. She'd married twice but never known what love even was. Duty pretty much described her life. Suddenly, she was asking herself duty to what.

"You are troubled," Connie said as she handed her the tea.

"I am worried about my daughter, of course." She knew it was more than that. Before she could say more, she heard the sound of boots and already recognized his sure step.

A few moments later, Taggert came into the kitchen. "Want some tea?" Connie asked him with a grin.

"I'll pass. Do you mind if we talk here, Connie?"

"Of course not, should I leave?"

"Not unless Mrs. Windsor prefers that."

"It's fine with me that you stay." She watched as he moved across the floor. For an older man, he moved with an athletic grace that bespoke a man who had lived a very physical life. She knew by the roughness of his palms that he had yet to settle into a sedentary life.

He took one of the chairs and turned it around to straddle it. "Wilson Potter has worked for Jonathan Cheshire for more years than he had for you."

"I don't understand."

"He's been on the payroll of the man who is a crime boss in Boston. Cheshire manages to avoid being arrested while those he sets to work take the fall. Your late husband, Irving Windsor, also worked for Cheshire."

"That's not possible. Irving was rich. He employed men. He didn't work for anyone."

Taggert shook his head. "It's how it looked. According to our source in Boston, Windsor was one of the many respectable fronts that Cheshire uses. You were born to wealth, weren't you, Mrs. Windsor."

"My parents were prosperous." She didn't like the way this was going.

"And your first husband, Thomas Lawrence was also wealthy."

"I suppose... What are you saying, that Irving married me for my money?"

"I can't say that. He could have loved you, wanted you as his wife, but he continued to work for Cheshire. At that point, he didn't have a choice. What would have happened if Cheshire had let you find out the truth that his shipping business was sinking in debt?"

"I don't know." She felt sick.

Connie went from the table to a sideboard, returning with a glass of sherry. "Drink this."

Frederica was not much of a drinker, but she took the glass. Sipping the liquor, she tried to get her head around what he was telling her.

"Here's the thing, Mrs. Windsor, Cheshire is good at using people and discarding them when they are no longer useful."

"What does that mean?" she looked up, met his dark gaze as he rose and walked to the counter, leaning his back against it, crossing one of his booted feet over the other.

"You've lived a pretty sheltered life."

"I ran businesses," she protested.

"Even then, a protected life. In that life there aren't people like Cheshire. How did your husband die?"

"Why does that matter?"

"Just tell me."

"He had a lingering illness. The doctor couldn't put a name to it but he became weaker and weaker, more in pain and then... well, one morning I went to check on him, and he was dead."

He let out a breath as he watched her. "I am putting some imagination to this, but if he ceased being useful to Cheshire. Maybe he felt guilty at what he was doing to you. Someone was there who could make sure he got sick, very sick."

"You don't mean Wilson?"

"Someone who could slowly poison him. Mrs. Windsor, my son, Asa poisoned my wife, his own mother. People do bad things. Sometimes for profit and sometimes just because they can."

She felt tears in her eyes and wiped them away. "I can't believe this."

"All right."

"Did this relate to why Catherine left Boston?" she asked as she worked to get her voice under her control.

"I find that unlikely. She'd have warned you if she had known. I think another possibility is more likely."

"And that would be?"

"Jace's Boston friend found out that Cheshire had Catherine's business decorating his home. I suspect when his wife died, he began to pursue Catherine. Just guessing."

"All of it is guessing, isn't it?"

"Some more likely than others."

"So she was trying to avoid him and decided to leave without telling me where she'd gone?"

"Possibly she was trying to spare you, afraid you'd do something that would cause you a problem if you knew she was being harassed. Remember this is all a guess."

She took another sip of the sherry as she tried to take it all in. "And Wilson in all this?" she asked finally.

"I don't know. He worked for Cheshire, but he also could have been loyal to you. Do you know for certain he had family in El Paso?"

"Just that he told me."

"Maybe when he comes here, he won't be alone."

"You mean he waited for someone?"

"Possibly. When you left Boston, how much warning did you give?"

"None. I just had to go and knew it. I felt Catherine was in trouble."

"So it's possible he had been told to wait there for help."

"I suppose it could be. Wilson sent a message that he will be in Tucson tonight."

Taggert walked to the window and stared out. "Okay, you need to pack your bags and go out to my sons' homes out on the desert. You'll be safe there. Spend Christmas with them."

"I should be here and ask Wilson about what you've told me."

His smile was crooked. "And you think he'd tell you the truth?"

She realized he would not. But why should she trust a man she'd barely met.

"I think Jeremiah is right," Connie said. "You won't be safe."

"Why would I be in danger?"

"If Cheshire wants Catherine," Taggert provided the answer, "you aren't needed, but your money would be. She is your heir, isn't she?"

"Of course. Wait are you saying?" She stopped again trying to think what he was telling her. "Wilson has cared for me. He wouldn't hurt me."

"He though does know where Catherine is, doesn't he?"

"He knew what I thought."

"I suspect they wanted you out here and an accident or even poison again would take care of any possible problem. You'd be far from the Boston police who might've investigated."

"And Cat?"

"She might not be safe either. You go out to my sons. I will head for the Circle O. Once the men down there, Cord, Sam, and Rafe, know the situation, they will make sure she's safe. When I talk to her, I'll know more what her part in this has been, why she left Boston as she did. More importantly, she won't head back here with no idea what's going on."

She considered that. "I can't let you do that."

"Mrs. Windsor, you can't stop me."

"I am going with you."

She saw him taken aback by that. "This is heading into very rough country, Mrs. Windsor. No buggies. It can be dangerous and I won't be traveling slow. You couldn't keep up."

"Of course, I could."

"You're a horsewoman?" His disbelief showed on his face.

"As good as any man."

He snorted. "I doubt that. Sidesaddle, I suppose."

"Of course."

"That is no country for skirts. It'd have to be astride. But it's impossible. I need to leave within an hour. No way. You stay with my sons."

She rose and walked to him staring up with what she knew was her stubborn expression. I will head there by myself or go with you. I won't not go."

"Like you'd know where it was."

"I am sure I can find a guide."

He cursed with a few words she hadn't heard but knew were strong exclamations. "It doesn't make sense," he said. "You don't even know I'm right."

"I feel you are. I wish you were not, but I feel you are. I need to get to Catherine. If Wilson is coming than likely so are others. Maybe they will try to kidnap Cat. She needs me… You will need me."

He gave a derogatory laugh. "Hardly likely."

"Fine. I'll go by myself." She turned to Connie. "Where can I buy a horse?"

Connie who had been listening smiled. "She's right, Jeremiah. She should go, and you will need her."

He stalked out of the room but then turned back. "I'll get you a horse. Buy jeans, heavy shirt, coat, hat, a change of clothes and be ready when I get back."

"I need to check out of my room."

He shook his head. "No, leave no trail. We go now. If they are getting in on the evening train, we want them looking for you first and wasting time before they head south."

"They?"

"He won't be alone." He looked at Connie. "Can you put together enough grub for three days?"

"I can."

He gave another hard look at Frederica. "I hope you change your mind. I'll be back in an hour."

"I can be ready sooner."

"I can't. I will bring canteens, bedrolls and a horse for you. If you get some sense while I am gone, you can have Del take you out to my sons' homes."

"I won't."

"Get some sense?" he asked with a faint smile.

"Change my mind."

"So be it." With that, he was gone

Jeremiah rode fast up to Ollie's place. "I need an extra horse," he said as he stepped off Blasted.

"What kind?" Ollie asked. One thing Jeremiah liked about his friend, his questions were always to the point.

"Solid personality, good legs, not a stumble foot on a trail."

"How about him?" Ollie asked pointing to a sturdy looking quarter horse.

"Looks good. Got a name?"

"Buster for now. I picked him up this summer, been working with him. Smart and not easy to shy. You going to tell me what's up?"

Buster came when he was called, and they pulled him out of the corral to saddle him. As they worked, Jeremiah told Ollie what had happened, and where he was heading. "You ever been there?" Ollie asked.

"Not at the ranch itself but down that way."

Ollie chuckled. "How'd you figger to find it?"

"It's the other reason I came to you."

"Be right back." He went into the house, came back with a piece of paper on which he'd drawn a map. "Just watch when ya get to the fork here." He pointed. "The creek has a way of changin'."

Rose, Ollie's wife, came to the door, Royce behind her. "You aren't staying for supper?" she asked.

"No time." He looked at the boy. "He looks like he's feeling better."

Royce nodded. "Hate doctors," he protested.

"Who doesn't?" Jeremiah chuckled. He looked back at Ollie. "I would like you to let Cole know what's going on. I don't want to call him and take the chance someone overhears just enough."

"I can ride over there. So Christmas at the Circle O?"

"If they'll have me. I am counting on Ryker not holding a grudge." He grinned.

"They will have you, but he might." Ollie chuckled. "Give 'em my love."

Jeremiah smiled. "And you tell my family the same." He took the lead reins of the spare horse and nudged Blasted in the side and took off at a fast trot. He stopped at his neighbor long enough to ask her to feed Scamp while he was gone. Then went into his home and stuffed clothes in a saddlebag as he explained to Scamp the situation. "I won't be gone forever," he said feeling like a fool for talking to a cat.

Scamp meowed but jumped off the bed to head for the kitchen and the scraps Jeremiah put out for him. He wished he could keep the cat in while he was gone. It wasn't feasible, not when he wasn't sure how long he'd be... or if he'd be back. Something about this didn't feel right. Maybe this was that karma Vince's wife Holly talked about. He'd deserve it if it was. One way or another he had to make sure that Frederica and her daughter were safe. He carried two coats out and tied them and his saddlebags to the back of his saddle.

At Sicillas, he rode around back, hoping Frederica would have realized this wasn't smart. She came out wearing boy's jeans, a long-sleeved cotton shirt, long duster, solid looking leather boots, and her hair stuffed into a brimmed hat and carrying a saddlebag. His hope had been whistling into the wind. He understood it but didn't feel less reservations about it. Connie followed her out with two sacks of food. He dismounted and began securing everything on the two horses.

"I haven't actually ridden astride," Frederica as she climbed competently enough into the saddle. "I am sure I'll get the feel of it though." He handed her the reins, and she did appear to know how to handle a horse. She showed none of the fear or uneasiness he'd been expecting. This was the least of what she would be facing. He knew she had no idea.

"You sure you want this, Mrs. Windsor?" he asked giving her or maybe himself one last chance as he started them on one of the less traveled roads heading south. He didn't want anyone to see them and maybe tell those who would be asking.

"Don't you think it's time you called me Frederica," she said.

He hadn't expected that. He looked over at her to read her expression. "It's a pretty long name," he said.

"You could shorten it."

"To?"

"Oh, ma'am or madam or." She laughed.

"How about lady?"

"I like Frederica better."

"You ever been called Freddy?"

"Good Lord no." She laughed again. "Is that how you think of me as a Freddy?"

He wasn't about to admit how he thought of her. "Could be. You look like a boy in those pants with the hat pulled low and your hair hidden."

"A pretty old boy."

He glanced over again. Did she really not know how beautiful she was or was that fishing for a compliment? "Freddy would be safer for me to call you as we head down the valley." They were passing the last of the gardens along the Santa Cruz. In the distance, he could see San Xavier.

"Why?"

"We don't want your friend and his friends to hear tell of a Frederica heading this way. We want them to have to look for you before they head south too."

"You truly believe Wilson is a danger to me?"

"If Cheshire wants your money and your daughter, then you are an impediment. Did you ever wonder why McClure told you she'd come this far but not where she was?"

"No, I thought he was just a bad detective."

"I am only guessing, but it comes from years of knowing a lot of lowlifes. I think they wanted you out here where they could arrange an accident or whatever. You fouled them up when you left Boston before they could get plans in motion. I think that's why your man stayed behind in El Paso. He wired what to do and was told to wait there for reinforcements before he came on." He looked over to see if she looked frightened.

"Mr. Taggert," she said, "I didn't want to think you were right, but I fear you were correct and that Cat would be vulnerable and need the comfort I did when I lost my son and first husband, then when Irving died."

"Probably, and shouldn't you make that Jeremiah? At least when we're not around people but when we are, call me Taggert."

"Why?"

"Some won't look too close when it's a Taggert, won't want to take the chance I'd brace them over it."

"You have a reputation."

"In some places. The books more than me though."

"Did you like that or mind it?"

"I thought they were funny. Cole not so much. He was young enough to be that outlaw hero. Caused him some grief."

He watched how she handled her horse and felt approval. She had quickly adjusted to riding astride. Her hand on the reins was not tight, wouldn't make the horse nervous. "You set a horse well," he said when he was satisfied that she did.

"I rode when I could in Boston but always bridle paths. This will be something new." She smiled at him. "This is a good horse. Is he yours?"

"Nah, a friend of mine. He trains horses and let me borrow it."

"It's what you had to do that took an hour."

"Among other things." He debated telling her. "Recently I got a cat or more accurately a cat got me. I needed someone to feed him."

"A feral cat?" She sounded surprised.

He smiled. "Suits a feral owner."

She gave a little laugh. "Should I be worried?"

"Heading off with an outlaw?"

"Yes."

"I'd say it showed poor judgment."

She laughed again. "Or it might be the best judgment I ever showed."

He looked over to see what she meant by that, but she was looking straight ahead at the road before them. Whatever she meant, he was likely better off not knowing.

CHAPTER 5

Riding south as they passed others coming north, Frederica felt a thrill clear through her at the beauty of the desert. She had always enjoyed horseback riding, but this went beyond any experience in her life. On each side of the valley, there were mountains, tall ones to the east and lower ones to the west. As it grew darker, she wondered how long they'd keep riding. She would not protest and give him an excuse to leave her behind.

She had known she had to go and had repeated it to Connie as they began picking out what she would need. She had asked her new friend, "Am I crazy to go off with a man who has told me he's an outlaw?"

"Was," Connie had replied. "Jeremiah grew up a hard way in a hard land. He did what he had to do. He's a good man through it all."

"I hope so." She held a pair of boy's pants up to her hips.

"I know so. You can trust him and his judgment, and he will need you. He just doesn't know it yet." Connie had smiled with that enigmatic way she had.

Yes, she knew she had to get to Cat and get there with him. It hadn't been fear for her own life, despite believing the warning. It had been more like her leaving Boston-- a demand she move and move immediately. It was like nothing she'd ever known.

Now and then, he rode in front of her when passing a wagon, or several riders heading north, but generally, they rode side by side. He only occasionally pointed to something he thought she might miss. She learned he wasn't a talker. She liked that. She wasn't either.

"You need to stop?" he asked her as the sun began to sink to the west with a glow of pink, lavender and gold.

"I'm fine."

"Good. I know a good spot to camp that's two miles farther."

"I can do that." Although she'd never ridden for this many hours, her horse's gait was a good one. The beauty of the terrain kept her enthralled. When he turned them off the road to the west, she followed to what was an arroyo. "This should be safe," he said as he pulled his horse to a halt. She followed suit and dismounted a little stiffly. A couple of deep knee bends helped to right her back. For a sixty-year-old woman, she felt rather proud of herself.

"You just sit over there on that log but check for snakes first."

"Might there be one?"

"Unlikely this time of year. Most hibernate, but you never know. Take a branch or rock and throw it behind the log. The snake doesn't want trouble and will leave. I'll get the saddles off and hobble our horses. If you feel up to it, gather up some small sticks for a fire."

She didn't feel like sitting. Walking and gathering firewood suited her as a way to work out any remaining stiffness.

When he came to her, he formed a ring with rocks, squatted, and built the fire. She watched how he did it as she was determined to be helpful. He opened the sack of food that Connie and she had put together. It was simple and spare with canned beans, potatoes, bacon, bread, coffee, and even some butter. Unfortunately, eggs had been out of the question.

Half an hour later, he had used more rocks to form a platform on which he set a small skillet from his pack. Their meal half an hour later was more satisfying than some she'd had at elaborate restaurants in Boston or New York City… maybe not than Paris though. Nowhere had better food than Paris. Something about this with the night growing dark, stars brightly overhead, the fire at the center, it came very close.

"You drink whiskey, Mrs. Windsor?" he asked as he reached into his bag for a bottle.

"I've been known to imbibe a time or two," she said, ignoring her irritation that he was still using her formal name. He was clearly determined to keep a barrier between them. He handed her the bottle, and she took a sip, gasping a little as she handed it back to him.

"Guess imbibe is one of those city words," he said taking a slug from the bottle before he set it down and lit one of his cigarettes.

"I suppose. It means…"

"I know what it means." He stared into the fire.

She wasn't sure if she had hurt his feelings and tried to think of a way to undo her thoughtless words. "What will the people be like with Cat?"

"Good folks. Two brothers who didn't know they were until they were well grown. One on one side of the law and the other on the other, but now on the same side."

"How could they not know?"

"The West broke up a lot of families. In their case, their pa was a bounder. You know that word, I reckon." He glanced over before feeding some more small sticks into the fire.

"I do know what it means. They are close now if they wish to spend Christmas together. How does Grace fit into it?"

"Another of those Western stories. Grace's pa, only got her when she was nine, after her grandparents died and her uncle dropped her on the marshal. I didn't know any of them back then. I was living in Utah but heard the stories later."

"Are they friends of yours now?"

He gave a snort. "Not sure, but reckon I will find out."

"What did that mean? You are a very enigmatic man, Jeremiah." He might not use her name, but she liked the way his name rolled off her tongue. It was a good name, a strong name for a man with a strong body and a face with strong lines and crags. It was actually a very handsome face. She especially liked his mustache. Not too big or too small. Just right for a Western man, an outlaw or maybe something more.

"A few years back, I was hired to kill Sam Ryker. I needed the money is my excuse."

She could not restrain her gasp. "Then going there is going to be dangerous for you."

"It's hard to say. He and I made peace the same year. A kind of a truce maybe. I've seen the brothers a few times in Tucson, but never been to the Circle O."

"It's confusing. So, a big family for Christmas."

"Very. There will be kids all over the place and three families. Sort of like my own."

"I feel badly that you gave up your Christmas with your family for this."

"No choice as I see it, and there will be other Christmases with them… I hope." He took a long draw on his cigarette.

"What did that mean?"

He turned to look at her, into her eyes. "You of all people know life isn't guaranteed."

"I suppose that I do. I would not like to think you would be endangered because of Cat and me."

"It wouldn't be. It'd be to do what is right. You might find this hard to believe, but even men on the outlaw trail can have a code of honor, a belief in doing what is right."

"Yet, you said you were going to kill Mr. Ryker for money."

"I believed he was an outlaw like me. Seemed fair. Turned out he'd turned his life around, was married. You'll meet her at the Circle O. He even had kids. If I'd known it all or known why the woman wanted him killed…"

She interrupted. "A woman hired you for that?"

"Eventually, I learned that. Evil as the day is long. A real snake. Anyway, it turned out my oldest son was a good friend of Ryker's. It's complicated too. He stopped what would've been a big mistake, even assuming the three I sent to do it could have done it. Most likely they could not have, once I understood the measure of Ryker. I'd have lost a son if it'd have gone otherwise."

"I am incredibly confused."

He gave a little laugh. "How about we leave off talk of the outlaw trail. What kind of Christmases have you known?"

She sighed and stared into the fire. "Good when my first husband and son were alive." She described how she lost them and her own sinking into depression. "When Cat needed me most, I wasn't there for her, as I tried to get hold of our businesses, handle my grief-- more at the loss of my son than my husband, I am afraid. Then I married Irving and that was a mistake on many levels. For me, Christmas has been a time of duty or loss. How about yours?"

"Drunkenness," he said taking another long drag on his cigarette. "That's what it was when I was small. My father fought with his brothers. He was a mean bas—... man. Given how my second son had a brutal streak maybe it was in his blood."

"How sad. But now with your sons having their families, it's better, isn't it?"

"It is but not my doing."

She watched his dark expression as he fed more wood into the fire. "You carry around a lot of guilt, don't you?" she asked when she saw he'd say no more. She realized in that they were two of a kind.

"In my case, well deserved. A man chooses a trail, and he can't blame anybody else when it turns out to be a wrong one."

"He can turn around."

"He can try, but my daughter-in-law, Holly has a word for it— karma. Sometimes there has to be payback."

"Possibly there is, but don't bring it on yourself by creating it."

He turned then and studied her face, his own expression impossible to read. "That goes for you too."

"It does. So, we will have a jolly Christmas. We will make it that way. I wish I'd had time to buy gifts though. I feel badly going to strangers without something."

He considered that. "If you mean that, we could make a quick stop at a shop I know in Tubac. You'd have to keep that hat brim low, deepen your voice, Freddy." He smiled then as he reached out and lifted her chin, so their gazes met. "Can you do that?"

"Shore can, Taggert," she said trying for a deep voice.

He laughed. "That'll do."

That night, for the first time in her life, she slept rolled in a blanket, with saddlebags for a pillow, under a black sky filled with stars. There were more stars than she'd seen in her life. She had imagined Jeremiah was asleep until he said, "Makes a man feel mighty small."

She smiled. He had kicked out the campfire, so she only saw his faint outline. "A woman too."

"You a religious woman, Mrs. Windsor?"

"Not so much, and I hoped by now we'd gone beyond the Mrs."

"It's better not to."

"Are you angry at me for something? Is that why you won't use my name?"

"No… Just trying to protect you and me. I need a barrier here, ma'am, to never forget there is one." She heard the smile in his voice. She understood what he meant. With a night like this, mistakes would be easy to make. She didn't intend to stay in Tucson. She didn't want a man, not ever again.

"All right, Mr. Taggert," she said and rolled over to go to sleep. Unfortunately, sleep didn't find her. She lay there listening to the quiet breathing of the man beside her, only a few inches and two blankets away. In a nearby tree, she heard an owl hoot and then another, from farther away. A coyote yodeled from the nearby hill. She'd heard them before but somehow, sleeping out with them excited her. Taggert had been right. It would be far too easy to make a mistake with how she was feeling. Stirred by the raw beauty and the awareness that she was with the kind of man she'd read about, but never known. What would it be like to walk beside such a man? Strangely, her main feelings were, that she'd be proud. When she realized that, she forced her imagination away from it. She could not afford such a man based on what he would cost her emotionally.

As they rode into Tubac, its feeling was that of a sleepy little Mexican town with adobe and stone homes. Strings of red peppers, bright ornaments, ribbons and wreathes were on porches and in many windows. Jeremiah turned his horse in front of an adobe with an open door. "Josh handles Mexican and Indian crafts. Just don't pick out anything too heavy."

She dismounted. "Does my horse have a name?" she asked as she stroked her gelding's neck before tying his reins to the hitching post.

"He did… Uh, Buster, I think. Ollie was a little vague about that."

"Vague?"

"He'd been training him. Only got him this summer."

"He's a great horse with an easy to ride gait."

"I noticed that."

Inside the store was darker but then her eyes adjusted to the few windows and lit kerosene lamps.

"How you been, you old bast---"The man cut off his comment when he saw Frederica. "You got a younger son than I knew?"

"Hiring this kid for a job."

"You ain't back on the…" He stopped again.

"Just need some Christmas shopping, Josh. Something easy to pack."

Josh then got down to business, showing them scarves, silver and turquoise jewelry. Frederica realized then that she had only a small amount of money with her, thanks to Jeremiah's insistence that she not return to the hotel. Gifts would not be possible. Jeremiah reached into his pocket and pulled out a roll of bills. "Get what you want."

She had not expected him to have that much money. She nodded, and in as gruff a voice as she could manage told Josh that she would like four colorful scarves, five beautifully carved small carved animals, and a few sacks of hard candy. Jeremiah added two more scarves and silver and turquoise bracelets. "You wrap them?" he asked Josh.

"Sure can. Even got Gold paper."

She watched as he took care of that, and Jeremiah paid him. "If anybody comes by asking about me, you haven't seen me," Jeremiah said as Josh stuffed the gifts into a flour sack.

"Nope, not in years." Josh cackled. "Like old times."

"A little."

Once outside, Jeremiah tied the sack to his saddle. "I don't much like the look of those clouds he said pointing toward where dark thunderheads seemed to be building to the south. He stopped to buy more food, telling her to stay with the horses and not answer any questions if someone asked. He returned with another sack, handing her a biscuit from it.

"We're going to have to ride faster now to beat that storm," he said after he had mounted, and they both ate heading out of town and back on the road.

"We can't get to the ranch by tonight, can we?"

"Nope but there is an abandoned cabin, or was last time I was by this way, which we should make before the storm hits, that is if you are up to it."

"I am." She hoped.

The sun was just hitting the horizon when he again turned the horses from the main road to a narrow lane. A mile up it, she saw the cabin. A door hung loose from the hinges. It had a chimney and looked like an actual roof as the first raindrops fell.

"Wait here 'til I check for snakes," he said, returning soon and reaching up to lift her from her horse.

"I could have dismounted," she said, but she was incredibly stiff.

"I know. Go on in, while I take care our mounts. He untied the bags from the saddles and set them in the cabin, which she saw had a table and three chairs, a cot in one corner, none of which looked like they'd been used in a long time. She stretched to loosen her muscles then looked around for firewood as it had a usable appearing fireplace at one end of the single room. She wondered if it had a privy out back. It would be better than the bushes she had been using.

When he came in, he shook water from his hat and threw his soaked coat over a hook by the door. "I could fix that door if you want," he said.

"It's fine this way. I didn't find firewood."

He nodded as he picked up a kerosene lamp from a small cupboard nailed to the wall. He took off the chimney, raised the wick, and lit it.

"I should have thought to do that," she said.

"No reason you would. Not likely you ever found yourself needing one."

She smiled. "We do get power outages in Boston."

"There is a shed out back where I put the horses. I'll see if it has any firewood. Outhouse is there too. I checked it for snakes."

She smiled and followed him out, taking care of her needs before returning to the cabin. She had never felt dirtier but something about it was all right—a kind of clean dirtiness—earned in a way. In the cabin, he was kneeling by the fireplace building a fire. The masculine beauty of his form took her breath away as the fire slowly kindled. He had piled their saddles and bags a few feet from the fire. They would be able to lean against them and soak in the warmth. Outside, she heard the first crash of thunder.

"This is cozy," she said as the glow grew from the fire.

"Not much like your world though, is it?"

She smiled. "Not much." That didn't make it inferior but just different. "I had a question."

He dug into the food bag and got out the small frypan. "Shoot. Figuratively." He chuckled.

"I could shoot. I had a derringer before you made me leave it. I bought a .38 to take with me."

"Protection from the big mean outlaw?" he asked as he set the pan on the irons for that purpose and opened a can of beans to dump into it.

"You never know. About the question. You had a lot of money in Tubac."

"And you thought I'd not have any money, I hadn't stolen to get?"

"I just wondered."

He turned back to the pan and stirred it with a big spoon. "My Utah hardscrabble ranch where I raised the boys, turned out to be rich in minerals. Cole, when he went back to sell it, found out. He sold it to some bankers back East, and it set us all up."

"All?"

"I divided it with the boys, of course. Now Vince and Jesse married rich women, but Cole and Willy had more need of it. I didn't need much from it, I live a simple life. I figured I might need some going down this way, that's all."

"So, no outlaw spoils," she teased wishing she could see his face.

"Nope, that life was a poor choice if a man wanted to get rich. Most ended up dead or in prison."

"You knew other outlaws?"

"A few. Men beyond the pale work together sometimes on jobs. I wouldn't go so far as to call it making friends."

"And your sons never did it?"

"Only Asa, and he ended up as most do."

"That's good about the others. What do they do then?"

"Jesse is a cowboy, now has an adobe where he trains horses. Vince is a trader and helps his wife who does archaeology when it's safe to take their small ones. Cole runs their ranch for fine beef."

"Those are good ways to live."

"It is for those who want to live to be old." He gave a little laugh. "Old age is coming as a surprise to me. I never figured I would get here."

The crash of thunder seemingly overhead, caused her to jump.

"You don't like storms," he guessed as he dished out the beans into two tin plates, handing one to her.

"They scare me. The wind even more than the rest." It was picking up outside, howling as it beat against the cabin walls and bent the trees she could dimly see through the door. Again, the lightning flashed, and immediately the thunder boomed.

"It was good we had shelter," he said as he ate.

"I suppose you've been out in storms a lot, and it's not a big deal to you."

"Lightning storms are always a big deal. This had the look of a bad one. Snow in the mountains probably. It's unusual to get storms like this in the winter, but they come along now and again."

"And tomorrow, will we actually be able to get to the ranch?" She knew it had to be Christmas Eve day. She wanted to find Cat, take her into her arms, but after all, Christmas was just another day. She thought that to comfort herself. It wasn't just another day. It was a day for family to be together.

"Streams might be a little fuller but not enough to cause a problem. We will be there before nightfall," he said with confidence that made her believe it. "The storm will blow past in an hour or two. We'll get an early start."

"Jeremiah how do you know to get to the ranch if you haven't been there?"

"Ollie drew me a map." He took her plate. "There was a pump outside, I'll go see if I can wash up the pan and dishes."

"You'll be soaked. You might get hit by the lightning."

He smiled as he stood. "If it was my time, it could. It's not my time."

"How do you know?"

"I haven't got you to your daughter yet."

"I don't want it to be your time after you do that." He looked down at her, his dark eyes inscrutable and then turned to walk into the pouring rain.

She wasn't sure how long before he came back, but it seemed forever. She had fed more sticks into the fire to keep it going. "You were gone a long time," she said.

"I pulled up some dried grass for the horses. Not much, but with the oats I brought, it'll get them to the Circle O."

The storm had clearly passed onto the north as she heard the thunder but nothing overhead. She wanted him to hold her. She knew he wouldn't do it. She considered asking him to, but he was right, there was a barrier between them. She wasn't sure it could be broken down and unless it was, there could not be more between them. They were responsible adults... She felt tears at the corners of her eyes and brushed them away. Damn to being responsible adults. Maybe it was too late though in her life to make other choices.

CHAPTER 6

They rode into the Circle O ranch yard in the early afternoon. Jeremiah was not surprised to see the greeting party was three men with guns. "What are you doing here?" Sam Ryker asked.

"Catherine Lawrence here?" he asked as he dismounted and held her horse while Frederica stepped down.

"That your business?" Rafe Cordova asked.

"It's her business. This is her mother."

At that, women came out of the house with children at their skirts. "Mama," a lovely young woman shrieked, as she ran to throw her arms around her mother. "You're supposed to be in Boston."

"Can I explain inside?" Frederica asked looking back then at Jeremiah and then the other men. "Will it be all right out here?"

"You mean will we kill him?" Ryker asked with a sly smile. "Not yet."

"He's joking," Jeremiah said, not sure at all that he was. "Go on in.

Explain this to your gal."

After the women and children had gone back into the sprawling ranch house, Jeremiah said. "Mind if I tell you about this while I take care of our horses?"

"Not at all," Cord O'Brian said. The two tall men looked so much alike that it was still hard to believe they hadn't known they were brothers from first sight. "You can put them in stalls in the barn."

Jeremiah led the horses to where he was told and unsaddled Blasted while Rafe Cordova took care of Buster. "This looks like the horse Ollie has been working," he said as he curried the gelding.

"It is. I borrowed him for this."

"You mean stole?" Ryker asked.

"I said borrowed."

"Why the hell would you take a lady down here, just the two of you?" Ryker asked with that cold gimlet eyed look Jeremiah had seen many times with him.

"More like she took me. I tried to get her to stay with my sons while I came down, but she wasn't buying."

"She's not much like I'd expected," Rafe said, "not from what Cat's said. I expected her in a fancy dress with a ledger." He chuckled.

"She is a surprise all right," Jeremiah said closing the stall gate. "Here's the thing. Cat left Boston without telling her mother. Did she explain to you or Grace why?"

"She was being harassed by a powerful man there."

"Was she afraid to tell her mother?"

"Afraid what her mother might do. She admitted she hadn't used good judgment by just leaving. She didn't expect her mother would come after her. She was trying to be careful and not give away where she went until she felt safe."

"It's more complicated than she knows. Her mother hired a detective to find her. Bryce McClure. Mind if I smoke?" he asked as they all walked to lean on the corral watching the horses grazing at the far end. "We been trying to quit," Ryker said, "but go ahead, be rude."

Jeremiah chuckled and pulled out a cigarette and lit it offering the pack to the other three. They looked at it longingly, before they all took one. "I think we're going to need this," Cord said as he lit his.

"Now let's hear it," Ryker said in no friendlier a tone. "I am guessing it does not relate to Saint Nicholas and reindeer."

"Very clever of you," Jeremiah said unwilling to resist the crack or the tone he used.

"No fighting until we know what's going on," Cord retorted.

"When Mrs. Windsor told me why she was here, the detective, Bryce McClure didn't sound right. He tells her Tucson, but no info on who she met or even if she was still there. Then when she tried to contact him, he was unavailable. I asked Cole to find out more about him. Turned out Sheriff Trask had a friend on the force in Boston. McClure had many aliases and worked for a Boston businessman, Jonathan Cheshire, who travels both sides of the street. His more profitable side was as a major crime boss, selling protection, smuggling, and the usual."

"That's the man who was harassing Cat," Rafe said.

"It gets worse," Jeremiah said taking a long draw on his cigarette. "The man who set Mrs. Windsor up with that detective was her majordomo, a man called Wilson Potter."

"Cat mentioned him. He's been a big help to the family," Rafe said his own face growing more stern as this all began to sink in.

"He apparently, according to Boston police, also works for Cheshire. When Mrs. Windsor got to Tucson, he avoided coming with her by claiming he had family in El Paso and was coming later."

"Certainly possible," Cord said.

"It could be but another possibility is when Mrs. Windsor made a quick decision to leave Boston, there was no time for Wilson to contact Cheshire. He managed on his way west, at one of the stops. I am guessing he was told to wait for support and then come on. He was getting in two nights ago. I wanted Mrs. Windsor to stay with my sons while I came down to warn her girl. She wasn't buying and said she'd come anyway. I believed her, and so I took her."

"Whee," Cord said letting out a breath. "That is quite a story."

"If it's true," Ryker said with suspicion.

"And I'd have what reason to lie?" Jeremiah asked.

"I'm working on it." Ryker blew smoke away from him.

"Besides warning Cat," Rafe said, "what else did you intend to do?"

"Then I'd have gone back to find Potter and probably McClure on their way here. I doubt Cheshire would have come. His kind hire men for that."

"You'd brace them by yourself?" Ryker asked with a skeptical tone.

"I figured one of you would go with me."

"How would you recognize the men?" Cord asked.

"I got a general description, but what are the odds of three or four strangers riding out here?"

"How would they know Cat was here," Rafe said.

"Several ways. Although he never showed up in Tucson, as best I can find out, he had to have a source there. I believe he knew she had gone out to your place."

"Why not tell her mother?" Cord asked. Jeremiah was unsure how much he believed anything he'd said. He didn't much care either.

"It's guesswork," he said, "but I think Wilson Potter killed her second husband by poison."

"You'd know about that," Ryker snapped.

"Shut up, Sam," Cord said. "I get it you'd be a little testy toward a man paid to kill you."

"A little."

"But it's been a few years, and he did try to stop it."

"Eventually."

Cord looked back at Jeremiah. "Tell us why you think he'd want her in Tucson."

"Most likely to kill her and leave her daughter for Cheshire. I can't see any other reason to have her here, but not tell her where to find Catherine. I am open to other possibilities."

"No, that's figuring it pretty fine," Rafe said. "From what Cat has told Grace and me, it makes sense in a pretty ugly way. Cheshire was also involved in kidnapping women for the slave trade. What she learned about him terrified her."

"I still don't figure why she didn't tell her mother," Jeremiah said.

"She said she was afraid for her. Cheshire is a powerful man, but she knew her mother would try to stop him. She is a strange young woman," Rafe said, "with visions and… purposes that go beyond this side of the veil. I don't think she told us all of why she had to come and so quickly without telling her mother." Rafe smiled as he watched Jeremiah. "You don't sound surprised by that."

"After Connie, nothing much surprises me." Jeremiah threw his cigarette to the dirt and ground it out with his boot. "Look, I did what I came here for, and you will keep them both safe. I can leave now and camp along the road out here-- waiting for them like I planned."

"What's the soonest they could get here?" Cord asked.

He had been considering that. "Potter and whoever met him in El Paso were getting in the evening of the 22nd. Keeping Mrs. Windsor from going back to the hotel, I hoped he'd waste time, trying to find her in Tucson, before he'd realize she wasn't there. Heading south, we took the old road out of Tucson, avoided being seen. It helped her looking like a boy.

"He'd spend that night and maybe some of the next day asking, looking around, he can't know she came here, but he knows where Catherine is. I'd put chips on that. I think when he can't find her mother, he'll come after her. It'd take him time to get together horses and grub. That puts him heading south late the 23rd or even the 24th. I don't see him making it out here before the 26th. He might have some trouble finding this ranch unless he hired a guide. I don't think he'd do that—to avoid leaving his own trail."

"They're likely to all be Eastern men," Cord said staring at the horses that were now coming up to see what they wanted.

"Slower going for them. You made good time with Frederica," Rafe added with a little surprise in his voice.

"Surprised the hell out of me. She's a good rider, sits a horse as well as any man. She's game too. Nothing like I expected when I agreed to take her." He had figured she would slow him down. She had not.

"You figured the timing pretty tight," Ryker said with grudging approval, "not that I am surprised after all your years on the outlaw trail."

Jeremiah grinned at that. "You managed a compliment and insult in one sentence. Not bad."

With a crooked smile, Ryker nodded his appreciation.

"Then let's go in the house for Christmas Eve," Cord said. "The kids get their presents Christmas morning. Just to be on the safe side, I will have one of my hands take turns keeping an eye on the road."

"I should do that," Jeremiah objected, "and wait for them a mile before the branch in the trail. Safer to keep them far away from your womenfolk and little ones."

"And kill them all or capture them? What'd you have in mind?" Ryker asked again with the sarcasm in his voice.

"Depends on how many," Jeremiah said, meeting Ryker's gaze. "One alone, and capture is a possibility. More and the odds aren't so good that one can stop them-- short of killing them all." And likely getting killed himself, considering he wasn't as young as he once was and not as fast.

"You two quit sparring," Cord reprimanded. "I want some time to think this out. And..." He looked at Jeremiah. "Don't tell me anything about killing. I might not still be a marshal, but I'd have to turn you in anyway."

"Fine, I'd ask them nicely to turn around, and I am sure they would," Jeremiah retorted.

Ryker chuckled.

"More like it," Cord said. "I think you should spend Christmas with us. Priscilla always says the more the merrier."

"I don't like intruding." That was the truth. He was still uneasy being with his own sons for such gatherings.

"It's not intruding. It's bringing Cat her mother and doing what you could to keep her safe. That makes you family too," Rafe stated firmly.

"Sure, take a rattler in, and he likely will turn friendly," Ryker jibed.

"I need to get something from the barn," Jeremiah said, surprised that he actually liked Ryker. He was more like him, than the younger man probably wanted to admit. No wonder Ollie was so loyal to the one he considered a son. He returned to the others with the sack of gifts Frederica had wanted to buy.

"What's that?" Cord asked.

"Gifts. Mrs. Windsor didn't want to come empty handed at Christmas."

"A store clerk, who might tell others he'd seen you?" Ryker asked again with suspicion.

"A friend."

"They sometimes turn on a man," Ryker snapped.

"This one won't. I doubt they'd think to check in Tubac, beyond the grocer or hostler anyway."

Cord nodded. "That's true. All right, let's wash up, and go on in." He smiled. "It's Christmas Eve. No more talk of guns and bad men. This is time for good food and tree decorating."

"Sure," Ryker said with an ironic smile. "We kill tomorrow."

"Nah," Cord said. "We'll save that for the day after Christmas."

Rafe laughed and Jeremiah knew that if it was needed to protect Mrs. Windsor and her daughter, they'd do that. He still considered his own plan better-- to meet Potter, and those he had with him, away from this good family. Stray bullets didn't show favorites.

Frederica was impressed by the O'Brian home. In one corner of what appeared to be a great room was a large pine tree but it was not decorated. Children and young adults were sitting at a table and stringing popcorn and cutting out paper snowflakes. Cat had introduced her to them all, but she was not finding it easy to keep track of who was who.

"We decorate Christmas Eve," Priscilla O'Brian said. "It's been a tradition."

"A lovely one," Cat said at her side, still with an arm around her.

"It is very lovely," Frederica said.

"I can't believe you are here," Cat said again.

"I would like to tell you all more about why," she said as she looked from Priscilla and Grace to Abby.

"In the kitchen perhaps. Would you like tea?" Priscilla asked.

"I would love some."

In the kitchen, she was introduced to Rosita who helped in the kitchen as well as her small daughter, Valeria, who played with her dolls in the corner by the stove.

"The ones, who know, say we might have a bit of snow Christmas morning," Priscilla told her as they all settled at a long table. The kitchen was a large room that felt warm and appealing. Sitting there, it seemed strange to think of murders and those who would hurt others, but she explained the story as best she knew. She finished with, "It's not all proven, but it makes sense. I can't believe I didn't see it long ago regarding Wilson."

"He was very good at pretense," Cat said. She had swept her long red hair back into a ponytail. "I had a hint once when I was hanging some new paintings in Mr. Cheshire's parlor and suddenly there was Wilson. He said he was there for a charity, but he seemed uneasy."

"I wish you had told me."

"I was afraid you'd be endangered by it once I understood how determined Mr. Cheshire was for me to marry him. I thought if I left, he'd have no further reason to bother you. Nothing he was doing, that I knew of, was against any laws."

Frederica sighed. "He apparently had been involved with us long ago, from my marriage to Irving. I was too wrapped up in my misery. I didn't pay attention to what I should have." She met Cat's gaze. "I wasn't there for you as I should have been."

"Of course, you were. I knew you had to take care of Mr. Windsor when he got ill. I never imagined he might've been poisoned."

"Who does such things," Priscilla said nodding as she sipped her tea. "We expect the best from others and are too often disappointed."

"We can only start from where we are," Abby said. "Speaking of that, I imagine you'd like a change of clothing and a bath."

"A bath?" she questioned with amazement. "Is such a thing possible?" She laughed. She'd only been out of civilization a few days, but it felt forever as though her world had turned over in that time.

"We have hot water," Priscilla said, "and a generator gives us electricity. If you can believe it, we have electric lights to put on the tree thanks to that. Candles were so dangerous."

"Then I'd love a bath. I only brought another pair of pants though and spare shirt. Jeremiah insisted we leave with no chance for me to return to the hotel."

"He was probably wise given the situation."

"I had your Christmas gift there," she said to Cat.

"We'll be back, and you can give it to me then. "I mailed yours to Boston." She laughed. "I did it though from Dallas on my way here to avoid Cheshire or his men finding me or coming to Grace's. I hadn't expected we'd go down here for Christmas."

"We like the whole family to be together," Priscilla said. She put out a hand to help Frederica rise. "I think you are about the right size for one of Alice's dresses. Even at fourteen, she's taller than me by several inches and slimmer." She laughed. "I'll gather up your change while Abby shows you to the bath."

Half an hour later, Frederica was leaning back in the tub and savoring the hot water, perfumed by lavender even as it cooled a little. She had washed and rinsed her hair, bundling it in a conveniently placed towel. She wasn't ready to leave the water.

She thought about Jeremiah and wondered how the men outside had taken his story. From what he'd told her, they were all used to guns. She had heard no shots, no loud arguments. That was encouraging. The problem was what happened next. Was Wilson going to show up at the ranch, and if he did, when would that happen?

As she reluctantly left the tub, let it drain as she dried her body, she considered how Jeremiah had held her away from him on their way south. At the time, she had understood and felt it was for the best. She no longer felt that way. He might see barriers between them, but were they any that were real? Maybe he wasn't attracted to her. She was an old woman. Although she was still slender of build, her skin wasn't fresh and dewy, she had gray in her hair. He was such a handsome man. He could have much younger women. Maybe her age was the barrier.

As she dressed in a pretty blue cotton gown, she remembered the ride south and how she had felt—more alive than she'd ever known. That wasn't just the beautiful scenery. It was the man, she had been with.

Except, was what approached dangerous enough to threaten Jeremiah's life or for that matter the men on this ranch? They were good people. It seemed wrong to let her mistake endanger them. She should have paid more attention to a businessman she had more or less barely considered. Some businesswoman she was.

Buttoning pearl buttons, she looked in a mirror. Fortunately, there was a comb by the sink, and it enabled her to remove the many tangles before she tied her still damp hair into a knot on top of her head. She studied her face, wishing she had met Jeremiah years earlier when she had more to offer. Still years earlier, he would have been an outlaw, and she couldn't have lived with a man who lived such a dangerous life—even if she overlooked the fact that outlaws robbed innocent people.

No, any chance she had with him would be this year and now. However, it would take her making the first move, as she was sure he never would. She'd never had to try to entice a man. She was unsure she knew how—especially not as insecure as she was about her looks.

Walking into the parlor, the men were sitting and drinking what likely was whiskey. Jeremiah looked none the worse for wear, so he hadn't been in a fight over this. She wanted to ask what the plan was except the children, who varied in age from young adults to children, might be upset by something dangerous at a time they probably looked forward to all year.

"Would you like some sherry?" Priscilla asked and she nodded, forcing herself to look away from Jeremiah. She did not want to reveal her growing feelings for him. That would be embarrassing since it was likely unrequited in terms of any sort of reciprocation.

A tall, dark-haired and very handsome young man came through the door. Abby rose and grabbed in a big hug. "I was afraid you wouldn't make it."

"Not a chance," he said with a laugh.

"Frederica, this is our son, David. He's a photographer."

David smiled at her as he took her hand. "I'm still an apprentice," he said.

His father, Sam Ryker, rose from a chair and gave him the kind of bear hug that lifted him off his feet. "Good to see you, son."

"You too, Pa." The young man looked then at her and then Jeremiah. "Didn't expect to see you here," he said as he accepted a shot glass of whiskey from Cord O'Brian.

"Last I saw you was Cole's wedding." Jeremiah looked at Frederica for the first time that she knew. "He was the photographer that day. Took some great shots."

"I tried." David smiled with clear pleasure.

Alice came to Jeremiah. "Will you cut some snowflakes, Mr. Taggert?" she asked.

He gave a little laugh. "Who put you up to that?"

She giggled. "Well, Mama did suggest it."

"Sure, I can do that," he said and went to the table where paper was being folded and cut to form beautiful flakes. The rest of the adults were soon coerced into joining as well as Frederica. She found herself beside Jeremiah as he cut intricate little holes in his future snowflake.

"You have done this before," she said as she watched him open it up.

"Years ago. My mother liked handcrafts." His expression was dark as though the memory was not good.

"I've never done it, but I am willing to try." She picked up scissors and managed an almost respectable snowflake. "Priscilla said it might snow."

"Feels possible. Something we don't see much at Christmas in Tucson."

"Boston has a lot of it, of course." She felt foolish to say it, but she wasn't sure what to say. They were in many ways strangers and yet…

The decorating of the tree was begun with Cord stringing globe lights with a star atop the pine. Then everyone added their stars as well as picked what they preferred from boxes of ornaments. When decorated to everyone's satisfaction, Cord plugged the lights into a socket, and the tree became almost magical.

"It is beautiful," she said thinking it was the most beautiful tree she'd ever seen. Simple with strings of popcorn and handmade decorations, mingled with the glass globes. It spoke of family and history.

Dinner was a delightful soup with loaves of bread. She refused dessert as she felt more stuffed than she usually let herself get. "It will be turkeys tomorrow," Priscilla told her. Cord and Jesse shot two on the ranch, young, tender birds they were."

"Sounds wonderful."

The family adjourned to the parlor where they sang carols while Priscilla played the spinet. Although she felt exhausted when she climbed the stairs to the room she had been given, Frederica never remembered a better Christmas. If it was not for the possibility of what awaited them, the unresolved risks, she'd have been happier than she remembered in years. Only one thing could have made it better.

CHAPTER 7

J eremiah slept in what was a bunk room used by the hands. Cord had given most of them time off to be with their families, so he only shared it with one other man, who was clearly Yaqui and spoke little English. That was fine with Jeremiah as he was in no mood to talk. He lay long after all around him had quieted, as he tried to think what he could do to fix things for Frederica and her daughter.

Killing never settled anything but sometimes it was the only way. Or was it? It seemed Christmas was a lousy time to be thinking of shootings. When Frederica and her girl went north, he had to be sure nothing awaited them. If they stayed at the ranch until New Year's, he could take care of Wilson and whoever he brought with him. Maybe he could convince the man to head back East, that anything he was planning would not work. He didn't believe that, but he had to consider it.

He slept only a few hours, but for him, that wasn't a problem. Using the outdoor shower, he cleaned up with the cold water before he returned to the house where breakfast smelled delicious. "You almost missed the gift unwrapping," Priscilla said handing him a cup of coffee.

"Couldn't have that. I wish I had something though to give."

"We understand."

In the parlor the kids were gathered and looking impatient. Frederica was sipping coffee and sitting by her daughter. He saw that the gifts Josh had wrapped had found their way under the tree. When all were seated, the gifts were brought to each by David, whose duty, this had apparently always been. There were oohs and awws with much appreciation for the gifts Frederica had managed to find with something that pleased everyone.

"I wish I had your gift here," Cat told her mother.

"You are my gift," Frederica said hugging her tightly.

Jeremiah walked outside after breakfast to smoke a cigarette and consider his options. Ryker joined him and took a cigarette when he offered. "You aren't staying, are you?"

"No. They'll be safe with you all."

"I saw how you looked at her, and she looked at you."

Jeremiah took a long draw on the cigarette. "It doesn't matter."

"Since when? Don't tell me you got ethics late in life." He chuckled.

"Since you said not to, I won't."

"I will tell you something you should already know by your age. It's never too late, when a good thing comes along."

"It hasn't come."

"Taggert, I won't argue with a man who is determined to make a fool out of himself and throw away something good."

"Good."

Cord came out followed by Rafe. "So, what's the plan?" Rafe asked as the four of them smoked.

David joined them. "You four are plotting something. What is it?"

"How do you know?" his father asked him.

"I know."

"Might as well tell him," Cord said. Jeremiah laid out what he knew and what he surmised.

"Actually, I think I might've seen your men when I left Tucson," David said. "I stopped at Sicillas. Three men were there. One was asking questions about a woman who had disappeared. That guy and one other wore Bowlers. The third looked like a hired gun to me."

"I am sure they got nothing there," Jeremiah said. "What day was this?"

"Saturday evening. I didn't stick around to listen to what all was said, as it was nothing to me, or so I thought."

"So that would mean they couldn't be here before tomorrow as they aren't likely to ride as fast as David did," Ryker said giving his son one of those fatherly looks that said be more careful.

"So, we enjoy our dinner and head out in the evening," Cord said.

"You don't all go," Jeremiah said. "I don't want your family time ruined."

"No, we don't all go," Ryker agreed. "With just three, Taggert and I can handle it. If it got by us, then the three of you are insurance."

"And why don't I go or Rafe?" Cord snapped.

"Because you two are too much on the side of the law," Ryker said with a chuckle. "If something accidentally happened, you'd feel you had to report it."

Jeremiah saw neither could argue with that. "I am not though," David said. "I will go with you. I'm good with a gun. You told me so yourself."

"You are not going," Ryker said, "because your mother would shoot me if I let you."

David growled but didn't argue further. Abby Ryker was clearly a force with which to be reckoned by father and son.

"It's settled then," Jeremiah said not really wanting Ryker either, but he wasn't going to stop him.

"Not really," a feminine voice said and for the first time he realized Frederica had come out and heard the argument. "You will need me."

"Are you insane woman?" Jeremiah asked turning to glare at her.

"How will you be sure it's Wilson and maybe McClure?"

"By their Bowlers."

"Not like others could not wear that kind of hat. I will be going. This was my fault. I won't let someone else fight my battles."

The other men disappeared back into the house, leaving Jeremiah to argue. He did not want her to go. He knew why. He didn't want to take the chance that stray bullet might hit her. He didn't want her hurt. "You are not going," he said looking out into what looked like the beginning of snow flurries. He took a long draw on his cigarette to steady his nerves, not for the battle that might lie ahead but for dealing with her knowing how he was beginning to feel about her. He had to keep a distance if he wanted to get through this. Soon, she'd be on her way back to Boston, and it'd all be easier.

"I am going with you," she said and she put up her hand to touch the bristles on his cheek. He hadn't shaved in a few days, and they were forming a beard. "I think you should shave for the dinner," she said brushing her fingertips along his jaw.

"I didn't bring a razor."

"I am sure there is one here you can borrow."

"Don't need it for what lies ahead."

"All right, have it your way." She moved those fingers to the other side of his cheek and turned his head so he looked at her.

"You aren't making this easy," he said.

"I don't want to make it easy. I want to make it impossible."

"It is impossible." He looked down and met her gaze. He saw in her eyes something he hadn't seen in a woman's in years, maybe ever.

"It's not impossible, Jeremiah. We just didn't stop to think how possible it was."

"You know better. There are a thousand reasons."

"Is one of them that you find me unattractive or too old?"

He saw the vulnerability in her eyes. He didn't want to, but he levelly met her gaze. "You are the most beautiful woman I've ever seen." He meant it. She was one who had aged into a fine wine, like old silver with a beautiful patina from having been polished and used so many times. He'd never wanted a woman more, a woman he could not have.

She smiled. "There are no reasons then. Kiss me, Jeremiah. I want you to kiss me."

Before he could make up his mind, Priscilla came to the door. "Sorry to interrupt, but dinner is ready." She had a smile on her face as they both turned toward her. He knew Frederica was flushed and guessed he was too.

Throughout the dinner, which was beautifully prepared, he knew it had to be delicious but his mind was on what she had said and what he knew was the right thing to do. Priscilla had set them next to each other, which didn't help as he felt her proximity like an energy that touched him in ways he'd long forgotten—if he'd ever known.

Then there was dessert, pumpkin, apple pies with homemade ice cream. Finally, it was time to leave the table. He tried to think of the right words to tell Frederica that what she'd suggested couldn't be what she wanted. More than that, she was not going with him to confront her hired man, and whoever was with him.

Outside it was snowing lightly as he went out for another cigarette. She followed him, wrapped in a wool shawl. "I'm cold, Jeremiah," she said, "warm me."

"God, do you know what you're doing to me, woman?" He felt his arms go around her as though they had a will of their own.

"I certainly hope so. I am not very good at this." She leaned her head against his chest.

"You are a rich woman from back East. I am a retired outlaw. Does that sound like much of a combination?"

"It depends on who the two are and what they want."

"And what do you want? You are going back East."

"I wouldn't have to or maybe just to sell what I own there. No, I could get an agent to do that. Cat says she is not returning."

He gritted his teeth against the temptations surging through him. He wanted to think it was possible. He knew it wasn't. "You're caught up in the romance of Willy's books?"

She laughed. He felt her breath against his skin, and then she looked up. "Am I?" He bent then and lightly claimed her lips. Just a kiss. He could have that much. Her arms came up around his neck, curling into his hair. "I told you to shave," she said with a laugh when he released her.

He kept trying to think of why this could not work. Suddenly he wasn't sure. "You can't come with me," he said as he released her.

She sighed. "I want to come."

"No. I'd be worried about you and I can't afford that."

"You will come back."

"Of course." If he lived through it. "The thing is if they come a different way than we expect, you need to be ready. Can you be?"

She nodded and brought his hand to her lips. "The first time I felt your hand, I liked how you had callouses. You work hard, don't you?"

"It keeps a man active."

"How old are you?"

"Sixty-five."

"I am sixty."

"You look twenty years younger."

She laughed at that. "Is your vision starting to go?"

"Hopefully not."

Ryker came out. "You two need to quit schmoozing, and we should go." He had on a heavy coat, gun belts around his waist with two holsters.

"You can shoot left handed?" Jeremiah asked. He knew the man was dangerous. Obviously he hadn't softened.

"Border draw," Ryker quipped.

Jeremiah looked down at Federica. "Do we have a deal?" he asked her.

"I want a longer one," she said. He couldn't resist and bent to give her another kiss, this one firmer. Then he turned and left to saddle his horse. When he and Ryker rode out of the barn, she was watching from the porch, with Abby beside her. Both women looked concerned. Jeremiah forced it from his mind.

As they rode down the road, Ryker's stallion kept trying to nudge Blasted, who resented the movement and pushed back.

"Why the hell do you ride a stallion?" Jeremiah asked as he again forced his gelding to stay in line.

"I like irritating people and horses," Ryker said with a wicked grin.

Jeremiah laughed. "Just so you know."

"Your horse seems to be holding his own."

"His name is Blasted for a reason."

"This is Zeus."

"Figures." They both chuckled.

"So how do we handle this?" Ryker asked.

"You would actually ask me?"

"It was your idea."

"Then it's the usual—give them a chance and then start shooting."

Ryker laughed. "I might actually like you despite you taking a contract to kill me."

"I did try to undo that," Jeremiah reminded him.

"To save your son."

"That too."

"Okay," Ryker said, "it works for me. I expect us to sleep out tonight, and it to be midmorning."

"I agree."

Several miles on, they stopped at a place where the road narrowed. A perfect place to stop especially dudes with no real clue what they were up against—other than maybe the one David had described as a tough. With a small campfire, they drank from a whiskey bottle and laughed over past experiences when both had ridden the outlaw trail.

"And you took the risk of settling with a woman from the other side-- why?" Jeremiah asked with whiskey loosening his usual reluctance to ask anyone such an invasive question.

Ryker considered that for a few moments, as the campfire made such a conversation even possible between two men who had once been enemies. "Because finally I couldn't imagine living without her, if I had the choice. I'd have been easier to die than walk away from her."

Jeremiah lit a cigarette offering one to Ryker who took it. "I can see how that could be. Never before but now I do."

"You have a chance at a woman way out of your league. Is that fair?" Ryker asked.

"No."

"Right answer." Ryker chuckled. "Just treat her right all the days you get."

"It seems unlikely."

Ryker's laugh was louder. "Don't it just."

Frederica sat in the parlor watching the fire that Cord had earlier fed logs before going out to see to the stock who appeared to be restless.

"We had a cougar around here yesterday," Abby said as she joined her on the sofa. "Cats, unless they are desperate, won't attack a horse. The horses though don't like the scent and it riles them. Most likely it was hoping to get one of the chickens, but the coop is too strong for them to break in."

Priscilla sat across from them on a stuffed chair. "It's always hard when they go off," she said absently. "Cord wanted to go, but he said there were reasons for Rafe and him not to. He sent Jericho to watch the road nearer the house."

"Jericho is an interesting name."

"He's Yaqui. I guess you know that Rafe is half Yaqui."

"I hadn't thought and guess Cat never had either."

The young adults were playing Whist in the dining room—or so they had claimed, but she had heard --ha, a straight beats two pairs, so she wasn't totally sure.

"Are you in love?" Abby asked, totally surprising her, as Priscilla poured and brought them each a glass of red wine.

She had to consider that. "I don't know. I am not sure I ever was before. Maybe this is just desire." She laughed lightly. "I haven't felt that either before."

"Goodness." Priscilla giggled. "Then it's definitely time you do."

"But a man like him… How would that work out?" She was repeating his arguments, the ones she needed to rebut if she had any hope of convincing him that this could work. If it could.

"Nobody can answer that but you," Priscilla said perching on her chair and leaning toward Frederica. "I can only say what it has meant to my life. It made all the difference to take a risk with my heart for all it gained me."

"And what was that?

"Walking beside a man like Cord has many rewards—a feeling of pride most of all."

Frederica understood that better than she would have a week earlier. She looked at Abby. "You married a man who had been an outlaw, didn't you?"

"He still was when we met. He changed only after."

"You took a big risk then."

"I suppose so but I felt he was a good man despite the reckless life he led. The only real advice I have is be sure you do love him… and get good at a gun yourself." She laughed.

"Why?"

"Because such men often have enemies with long memories."

"You have both given me a lot to consider. Thank you."

She only realized Cat had been at the door when she said, "Mama, what is this about?"

"I am… uh interested in a man but have not known him well."

"Mr. Taggert?"

"As a matter of fact, yes." She tried to read her daughter's expression.

"He walks with darkness," Cat said.

"You mean he's evil?" She had come to respect her daughter's insights. Again, she wished Cat had trusted her equally in Boston.

"No, not that. Just he might draw it to him."

"So, you would not like it, If say something were to develop between him and me."

Cat smiled. "I want you to be happy. Only you can decide what that would be."

"I am trying to decide, and I am happy that you'd be open to whatever develops."

Cat stared toward the window into the darkness. As had happened before, when she'd seen that expression on her daughter's face, Frederica wonder if she was seeing or hearing something. Cat shook her head and smiled. "It is possible that my not telling you brought you here for a reason."

"I believe in such," Priscilla said. "Do you have a gun, Frederica?"

"In my saddlebag, not loaded, of course given your family and all."

"They all understand about guns. What do you have?"

"It's a .38 because Jeremiah would not let me retrieve my things where I had a derringer. And, yes, I know how to use it."

"Might I suggest," Abby inserted, "that you keep it loaded and closer, like in the pocket of that dress, it has a pocket specially reinforced for that very reason."

Frederica considered that before nodding. "I will.

CHAPTER 8

I n the morning, Ryker and Jeremiah had just enough campfire to make coffee before kicking it out to wait. A few snow flurries swirled on the breeze, reminding Jeremiah of the family decorating the tree and the paper snowflakes. He had known nothing like it, other than reading about such families. It made him want Ryker back at the ranch. He knew the caliber of the man though, and he'd not leave until it was finished. Ollie would never forgive him if the man he regarded as a son was killed.

"You think loud," Ryker said with a chuckle.

"I don't need you for this."

"Probably but you've got me."

"If you get killed, Abby will never forgive me, and Ollie will kill me."

"All possible, but it takes a lot to kill me."

Before Jeremiah could think up more reasons, they heard horses. They had hobbled theirs farther up the draw from where they'd slept. The riders approaching would not know they were there.

Jeremiah loosened his revolver in his holster and moved with Ryker into the road to assess who was approaching.

Two bowlers with the third rider wearing a flat brimmed hat.

"Far enough," Jeremiah said. The riders stopped.

"You have a problem, mister," first bowler asked, as the three drew their mounts to a halt.

"Not if you turn around." He was aware Ryker had come to stand at his left.

"It's a free road, ain't it?" Flat hat asked.

"Not for the likes of you."

"I will go get the sheriff," second bowler said.

Jeremiah studied him to determine if he was a risk in a gunfight. He was the back shooting type, which didn't make him less risky. He looked back at the one most likely to actually pull a gun as that man dismounted and stepped in front of his horse. Obviously, he was paid to get the other two past obstacles.

"It's not a lot of money to die for," he said as he saw the man's eyes flicker. He pulled his own hogleg, shooting as soon as it came level with the man's chest. A shot screamed past his head as the man fell. He shifted his gaze to first bowler. The man had turned white as he stared at Ryker. He flicked a gaze at him to see Ryker's gun was out and pointed at the two remaining men.

"We'll bury your friend," Jeremiah said. "He got a name for the marker?"

"Bill," the shaken man said.

"Turn around and be gone. Don't come this way again."

"I am worried about my employer," first bowler said. That meant he was Wilson Potter.

"You can worry about her back in Tucson," Jeremiah said. "You spend more time here, and you'll end up like your friend. Oh, and give a message to Cheshire." He looked at second bowler, who he guessed to be McClure, "From now on, he leaves the Windsor family alone, or he'll find money doesn't protect him for what comes next."

Potter turned even whiter.

"Yeah, I know who paid you and who you work for. My guess is your boss doesn't take to failure. If I was you, I'd head west, but that's up to you."

The shot that winged his shoulder came as a painful surprise, but Ryker's responding shot didn't as the second man, the one he figured was McClure grabbed his arm.

"I could've killed you," Ryker said, "maybe should have, but it's not too late to change that if I ever see you again. You're a coward and a back shooter. I don't take well to that sort."

"I am going to report this to the sheriff," Potter said.

"I doubt that very much, but go ahead," Jeremiah said. "You had your chance. Get out of here."

With that, the two turned their mounts and rode back down the road.

"He hit you bad?" Ryker asked when they were out of sight.

"Just a nick. I am too old for this game as I wasn't watching him, even though I figured him for what you said."

"Too old?" Ryker chuckled. "Yeah sure." He laughed again. "Did you get nicked on purpose, so you didn't have to dig a grave?"

The wound was beginning to sting, but it didn't amount to much. Together they took turns digging a hole and then tossing the miscreant into it. What bothered him more than having his hide nicked was that he'd not been watching the man.

"You likely saved my life," he said as they broke camp and rode back toward the Circle O.

"He wasn't a good shot, but maybe." Ryker laughed again. "Irony, I would say."

"Considering, yep. Thank you." The words came hard. He didn't like owing the gunman.

"I did it for Ollie and the pretty lady back at the ranch."

"Then I don't owe you."

Ryker chuckled. "Nope. You sure you don't want me to look at the nick. I see blood on your shirt."

"I've had worse with barbed wire."

"Miserable stuff," Ryker grunted. "I'll give you that."

Jeremiah glanced down at his shoulder. There was blood on his shirt. He'd have to change it before he talked to Frederica. He had things to say to her, mostly that would let her head back to her home or go with her daughter wherever he headed next. What he knew wasn't possible was what she had suggested wanting. There would always be somebody like McClure in his life. Frederica deserved more than he could ever give any woman. Maybe she'd already come to recognize that.

Watching the two ride into the ranch yard, Frederica stood with Abby and Priscilla. She had to wait as they headed for the barn first to take care of their mounts. When they walked up to the house, Priscilla had gone inside to finish up the supper.

"You look like you are whole this time," Abby said as Ryker came up to her.

"I am, but he got a hit," Ryker pointed to Jeremiah with his thumb.

"Need doctoring?" Abby asked. Frederica felt herself whiten at the sight of blood on Jeremiah's shirt.

"Nope," Jeremiah said. "It's nothing." He looked then at Frederica. "We need to talk."

"See you inside later," Ryker said as he followed his wife into the house.

Jeremiah stood with one booted foot on the porch step, the other on the ground. He looked ready to leave. She moved off the porch to stand where he had to look down at her. She didn't want to make this easy for him. She sensed, what he would say, she'd not want to hear.

"I killed the hired gun," he told her, his tone steely and his eyes narrowed. "Ryker winged McClure when he used a hideout gun. Your man might still be in Tucson when you return, but I told him that Cheshire wasn't likely to take well to failure. He might leave and head west."

"Or not?" She was not worried for herself but would there be more danger for Jeremiah?

"He is no gunman. I can't say I caught his measure. He could try to bluff his way with you when you go back, get you to not fire him."

"That's not possible. I will never trust him again after this. Do you think they really came here to kidnap Cat for Mr. Cheshire?"

"Hard to say, but anyway they are unlikely to show up here. You have time to think it through. Rafe will protect you if need be when you go back."

"You aren't coming?"

"It can't work for us." She heard the tone of finality to his voice. Did he regret that it could not?

"Because I am too soft?" she asked remembering what Abby and Priscilla had said to her.

"No because I am."

"I don't understand."

He let out a breath. "The truth is I don't want you near me."

"Because?"

"Isn't it enough that I don't?"

"I'd like a reason." He didn't desire her. That was the problem. She was too old. She understood even as she felt hurt. Too late for them.

"What happened today has happened before."

"This time you were protecting my daughter and me."

"Next time it'll be an old enemy. I never really understood before how a man might regret his choices, but sometimes there is no undoing them."

"So, it's because of you, not because you find me undesirable."

She saw him hesitate. If he lied, she'd know it. "It's not that. It's my life and what it's led me to be. I was an outlaw and that leaves a stain. The man I killed today is not the first. I didn't even feel regret when I did it." He stared beyond her to the corral. "I wish it was otherwise, but it isn't."

"Jeremiah," she said and stopped as she saw motion around the side of the house. Before she had time to think, she pulled out her gun. When she recognized it as Wilson, with a revolver pointed at Jeremiah's back, she fired without hesitation.

Wheeling with his own gun out, Jeremiah moved to where Wilson lay twitching. He kicked the gun from his outstretched hand. It was clear Wilson was dead. At the sound of the shot, the adults had streamed out of the house.

She had killed a man. She felt almost numb and only realized she was holding the gun when Jeremiah returned to take it from her.

"Are you all right?" he asked lifting her chin so their gazes met. She wasn't sure. She should have felt something. Wilson had come to kill either her or Jeremiah—maybe both. She'd had no choice in what she did.

"We'll take care of this," Cord said. "It was clear self-defense and not something I feel a need to report." While the men took the body to be buried, Abby, Priscilla, Grace, and Cat insisted she come into the house.

"Drink some sherry," Priscilla said handing her a small glass.

"I'm fine," she kept saying but evidently, they did not believe it, and she drank the sherry. It warmed her where she had felt frozen. She looked from her daughter to the other three women. "I am sorry this came to your home."

"It wasn't your fault," Priscilla said. "He brought it on himself. You had no choice."

"I'm just glad you took our advice," Abby added, "and carried the gun."

She was too. She sat as she tried to take it all in. She supposed someone should say words over Wilson's grave, but it wouldn't be her. The man had betrayed her and was going to murder Jeremiah and probably her. Maybe, there weren't words to send such a man on his way to wherever his soul was bound. She put her thoughts from him. It was over. What she wanted was to talk to Jeremiah, to assure herself that his wound was as insignificant as he'd said.

It was half an hour before he came into the house with the men. His gaze landed on her. She tried to read what she saw in his eyes.

"It's time for me to see to your wound," she said, expecting some argument, but he just nodded.

"Do you know how?" Priscilla asked her as she led them into the kitchen.

She nodded, and Priscilla got out unguents, whiskey, and linen strips for bandaging. She turned and left them alone.

"It's nothing," he said. "How are you?" Now she knew she saw regret in his eyes.

"I will be better when I wash that wound and see for myself that it's nothing."

He sat on a chair at the table and unbuttoned his shirt, sliding it off one muscular shoulder. The scrape was a long angry gouge, but it was not bleeding. She poured a little whiskey over it and felt some satisfaction at his wince. At least he could feel something. Then she applied the ointment. "It probably does not need to be bandaged," she said as he shrugged back into his shirt.

"You did what you had to do, but I'm sorry you had to shoot him," he said. "I know he'd been a friend." Before he could come up with more words, she sat on his lap.

"He was never a friend. I can't believe I was so blind to his true nature. Maybe he did kill Irving. When I saw him pointing that gun at your back, all I could think was I wouldn't lose another man." She had expected him to argue with her, but he said nothing. "Do you think McClure will be a danger?" She put her arms around his neck.

"I doubt it. He was most likely hired by Potter. He won't want to return to Cheshire as a failure. He'll nurse the wound Ryker gave him and probably head west for a new start. His type is a coward and won't buck the odds. It'll leave Cheshire to wonder what happened."

"Will he send more?"

"Could be but not for a while, and now you and Cat know what he is. It won't be so easy. I still can't believe you shot Potter. Was that a lucky shot?"

She knew her smile was a little shaky. "I enjoy shooting skeet, learned to use my derringer. The .38 that I bought at Sicillas isn't that different... fortunately."

"And you are not suffering for doing it?"

"Maybe there will be a delayed reaction but not right now. Do you suffer when you kill a predator or a weasel?"

"I am more used to this life."

"And I guess I am tougher than I knew."

He snorted with disbelief. "You have no idea," he said, then stopped. "I guess the truth is I don't know you as well as I thought."

"You don't. I have lived through losing two husbands and a son."

She saw him take that into consideration. "So, what do you want now with me?" She saw in his eyes that he expected her answer to use him as a momentary distraction and then be gone.

"Is your Tucson home big enough for two?" she asked with a smile.

"No closets and the answer is no."

"Then we will have to buy something a little larger."

"You don't mean move in together." His breathing had grown a little faster.

"I was thinking something more permanent but... aren't you supposed to ask me that question?"

"You don't mean you'd say yes if I did."

"I don't?"

"I need to think. Are you caught up in the romance of those damned books Willy writes?"

"Maybe in the beginning, but not after we rode south together. Jeremiah, I am tougher than I look, tougher than I knew. I think tough enough even for you."

He stared into her eyes. "You don't mean marriage?"

She laughed and bent to brush his lips with hers. "Don't ask me if you hope the answer will be no."

He shook his head. "I am having a hard time getting my head around this. We are an unlikely pair."

"Are we?"

"The retired outlaw and the rich widow? Doesn't work, even in a book."

"Depends on the book-- besides, I'm not just a widow or rich."

"Maybe you are an outlaw."

"Maybe that's so."

"I hope you know what you're doing."

"Do you?"

"Not a chance." He lifted her from his lap and stood in front of her, taking her hand. "I've never done this before—never figured I would, but…" He went down on one knee. "Frederica, whatever the hell all your names are, will you marry me?"

She felt her heart fill with warmth. "As soon as we can round up a pastor," she said with a nervous giggle.

He rose to his feet and pulled her into his arms. When he bent to kiss her, she met his lips with hers, eager for the kiss that was hard and demanding.

"You'll probably regret it," he said when he released her, "but I can't say I don't want you as my wife. I have never felt this way about a woman even though I was married twice."

"And neither have I. I want what we can have for as long as that's possible."

"And I don't have to go back to Boston with you?"

"I want our home to be in Arizona. So, let's tell my daughter, and the family here. I am anxious to get back to Tucson and plan a wedding... a very simple wedding, so we don't wait too long."

"I haven't said it in a lot of years and maybe never meant it back when I did. I love you, Freddy."

She giggled again, filled with joy. "I love you too, Mr. Taggert and am looking forward to adding Taggert to my string of names."

With that, they both laughed, and he kissed her again.

If you enjoyed this book, please consider doing a review for it. Reviews are so important for authors as a way to connect with their readers. It has been interesting adventure to write a series that began in 1883 and carries through to modern day descendants and how their lives are impacted by those who came before.

Book eight in the Arizona historical (Hunters Moon) series shares characters from *Outlaw Way, The Marshal's Lady, Forbidden Love, Rose's Gift, Echoes from the Past, Lands of Fire* and *Destiny's Call.*

There will be one more Arizona historical that will explain how the supernatural powers came to be in the contemporary series involving the Hemstreet family—*Mystic Shadows Books 3 to 7.*

www.ingramcontent.com/pod-product-compliance
Lightning Source LLC
Chambersburg PA
CBHW060645130626
46555CB00002B/969